Lock Down Publications and Ca$h Presents

DEATH OF A SIDE CHICK

A Gangster's Love Affair

A Detective Gordon Noval

Written By

LO-LIFE

First Edition 2026

Printed in the United States of America

Lock Down Publications
P.O. Box 944
Stockbridge, GA 30281
www.lockdownpublications.com

Like our page on Facebook: Lock Down Publications
www.facebook.com/lockdownpublications.ldp

Stay Connected with Us!

Text **LOCKDOWN** to 22828 to stay up-to-date with new releases, sneak peaks, contests and more…

Like our page on Facebook:
Lock Down Publications

Join Lock Down Publications/The New Era Reading Group

Visit our website:
www.lockdownpublications.com

Follow us on Instagram:
Lock Down Publications

Email Us: We want to hear from you!

Prologue

May 21st, 1993

School was finally over. Summer was there, and little Uniquha couldn't wait to get home so she could play with the new Barbie Doll set her daddy bought her for her sixth birthday. Technically, her special day wasn't until June 21st, but he always bought her gifts early—just another reason that she loved him so much.

Uniquha, or just plain old Unique for short, was an exceptionally bright, young lady. The Honor Roll was a recurring achievement. Sometimes, school bored her, causing her young mind to wander. She would picture herself as a great lawyer, solving big, important cases. She didn't have many friends, but she didn't mind. Her mom and dad gave her all the love and affection she needed.

The school bus pulled up and parked right in front of her apartment complex. Little Unique hopped right off, her Rugrat backpack strapped to her tiny frame. L.A. Lights flickered on and off as she practically ran toward her apartment.

As she rounded the corner, a money-green Monte Carlo almost sideswiped her as it fishtailed out of the complex.

Rrrrhhh.

"Awkk, awkk." Unique coughed as thick smoke from the burnt rubber clogged her tiny lungs. She waved her hand in front of her face, fanning the smoke away before continuing.

About ten feet from the front door, her steps faltered. Her heart began pounding in her chest. The wooden doorframe was dilapidated, hanging at an angle and barely holding on by a few screws.

Unique knew her mom was at work, but her dad was always home to greet her when she got back from school. She shook her head, refusing to believe something was wrong. Still, deep in her tiny belly, she already knew the truth.

As scared as she was, Unique forced herself through the doorway. “Daddy,” she called out meekly. “Daddy, are you home?”

No answer.

Her hands shook. Her body trembled as she moved further into the small apartment. The smell of wet metal was so strong that it nearly made her throw up. Her teeth rattled as she whispered a silent prayer. *Please let Daddy be alright.*

When she took tiny steps into her parents’ bedroom, her world came crashing down. Her dad, the man she believed was invincible, lay sprawled across the blood-soaked carpet. His eyes were wide open, a hole dead center in his forehead.

“Aaahhh!” Unique screamed until her tiny lungs burned.

Whether it was shock or pure refusal to accept what she was seeing, she stood rooted in that spot, screaming until her mom came home from work.

When Gloria Gordon saw what had become of her husband of ten years, her knees buckled. She broke down worse than her young daughter had.

Eventually, the police were called, and an investigation was conducted. Unfortunately, the detectives decided to close the case and file it as another unsolved murder. That decision was the straw that broke the camel’s back.

Gloria began indulging heavily in drugs to numb the pain, namely crack cocaine. Slowly but surely, her addiction began to affect Unique. There were no more pretty clothes and nice shoes, no more Barbie Doll sets or Easy-Bake ovens.

By the time Unique turned ten, her mother was a full-blown addict. Unique had to find a way to survive.

She grew to despise the detectives who handled her father's murder. In her mind, it was their fault her mother became what she was. Instead of turning to a life of crime in protest, she made a decision right then and there that she would become a great detective. Maybe one day, she would be the one to finally solve her father's murder.

December 12th, 2025

Rachel Willis said goodbye to her lover and slid her pregnant body into her two-year-old Honda Accord. Even though their relationship was essentially a secret, he never failed to make her feel like the most important woman in the world.

She was far from perfect. Rachel had demons from her past, struggles she battled daily. With his help, she felt as if she finally had a firm grip on her life and looked forward to building a future with him.

Chapter 1

"What do we have?" I ask one of the responding officers on the scene. He's a young Hispanic with a goatee and deep dimples. *He can't be over twenty-five,* I think to myself as he begins giving me details of the crime scene.

"Well, the victim's name is Rachel Willis. She's married, with a son at home and one was on the way."

"Was?"

"Yeah. She was pregnant."

I close my eyes, shaking my head in disgust, amazed at how cruel this world can be. No matter how many times I do this job, certain things will always get to me. "Around 4:15 a.m., a man by the name of Cyrus Mitchell was headed to work and noticed the victim's vehicle somewhat jackknifed on the side of the road. After pulling over to offer assistance, he discovered the victim stabbed to death in the front seat."

I walk over to the vehicle and peer inside. Rachel is sitting with multiple lacerations to her neck, chest, and stomach. *Whoever did this must've been angry.*

My eyes scan the immediate area. I spot a pack of matches from a seedy motel down the road called Speedy's. There's also a Houston Astros ball cap sitting on the passenger seat. I can't really tell, but I don't see any blood splatter. *There should be lots of blood.*

Sitting on the floorboard is what I assume to be the murder weapon lodged under the gas pedal. I call over the chief forensic officer, Sade Lockhart.

"Wassup, G?" she greets me.

"I need everything bagged and tagged as soon as you can. Run tests on that ball cap and cross-check it with the knife."

"Will do."

"What do you have so far?" I ask. At thirty-one, Sade is one of the best in her field. She's helped me solve multiple homicides, including a high-profile serial-killer case a few years back.

"Well, it appears the vic got out of the car and headed this way." Sade begins pacing toward the rear of the vehicle.

Hearing that Rachel stepped out of the car strikes me as odd, to say the least. Sade walks about fifteen paces, then stops. "Apparently, she was hit from behind and dropped right here."

I walk over to the spot she's referring to. "What makes you say that?"

"Well, look." She points to a patch of dirt. "The dirt tells the story. Plus, there are small amounts of blood. I checked the back of her head, and sure enough, there's a contusion."

"Okay, so you feel she was hit from behind, killed, then placed back in the car?"

"It's still too early to say, but that's my off-the-head analysis."

I give her a solemn nod, then head back to my partner, who's at the victim's car, doing his own inspection. He hears me approaching, looks up, and asks, "What are you thinking, Gordon?"

Detective James Carter and I have been partners for the last two years, ever since Holtkey was murdered by an apparent stripper on the southwest side of Houston.

At age thirty-eight, Carter is exceedingly handsome for a white man—five-foot-ten, 190 pounds, powder-blue eyes, with a firm backside. It's been months since I've had some good loving, and every time we're around each other, my coochie starts whining for attention. *Too bad he's married.*

"Well, according to Sade, she believes the victim was outside of the car, en route somewhere, when she was hit from behind. There's blood at the site, consistent with that theory. So, either the victim was killed outside the car and placed back inside, or she was placed inside and then stabbed. Due to the lack of blood in the car, I'm suspecting the former. Either way, she had to have felt comfortable with her attacker to turn her back on them. Do we have a list of contacts? Close friends? Family?"

"Actually, we do. She was married to Edward Willis, a twenty-eight-year police veteran who was discharged due to excessive force. They'd been married for eight years and have a five-year-old son together," Carter informs me.

"Let's go pay Mr. Willis a visit," I say, heading toward our police-issued sedan.

"Let's go."

As we're heading down Highway 90, I spot a brown and beige building off to the right side of the road. The neon sign reads *Speedy Motel.*

"Pull over real quick, Carter."

He turns into the parking lot. There are only five vehicles across the entire lot. I'm sure one belongs to the owner or manager. Carter takes note that it's a motel, looks at me, and smirks. *I wish.*

"I spotted a pack of matches in Rachel's car with this motel's logo and name. Maybe she came here last night," I explain.

"Of course. Why else would you want to take me to a motel?" he chides.

"Shut the hell up," I say as we both get out of the car. The first thing I do is take note of the security cameras. As of now, I only spot two. One is close to the office, and another is at the entrance when you first turn in.

We step into the lobby, and an olive-skinned Pakistani man greets us.

"Welcome to the Speedy Motel. How may I help you?"

I produce my credentials. "I'm Detective Gordon, and this is my partner, Detective Carter. We'd like to ask you a few questions." I can tell he's nervous in the presence of authorities. *Good. I'll use that to my advantage.*

"Okay, Detective. What is this all about?"

"We're investigating a crime and wanted to know if you happened to see a late-model, navy-blue Honda Accord at your establishment recently."

The manager closes his eyes as he scrolls through his mental Rolodex. "Uh, yes. Last night, a white woman buy room while Black man wait in the car for her," he finally remembers.

"Do you remember what the Black man looked like?" Carter asks, hope saturating his voice.

"No. He stay in car the whole time."

Carter sucks his teeth in frustration.

"What about the security cameras?" I ask, already suspecting I know what the answer will be. He looks around nervously, afraid to meet my eyes. "Excuse me. Right here." I slam my hand on the counter to get his attention. He snaps his head in my direction.

"The cameras? Uh, cameras don't work. I have to get them fixed," he mutters. *Un-fucking-believable.*

"Are you serious? So, you mean to tell me you're running a business with no security cameras?" I ask, more than a little perturbed.

"Well, we have cameras. They just don't wor—"

"Motherfucker, that's the same thing!" Carter explodes.

I grab hold of my partner and push him out the door. "Come on. Let's go." As we're heading out, I look back over my shoulder. "We'll be back soon, and you better have the cameras fixed, you crooked motherfucker."

We get in the car, and I slam the door shut as we sit there, exasperated. This could've been the smoking gun—footage of the victim and a possible killer together moments before the homicide. It would've made the job that much easier. I take a deep breath, turn to Carter, and say, "Let's go see what the husband has to say."

Rachel and her husband, Ed, stayed in a four-bedroom brick home in Atascocita. According to the file, Edward Willis is a retired veteran with a long list of excessive force complaints and outright police brutality.

Ed grew up in Fifth Ward—Coke Apartments, to be exact. After watching most of his friends fall to gun violence, he decided to become a police officer. The only problem is that you can take the man out of the hood, but you can't take the hood out of the man. With a badge, a gun, and a license to kill, Ed became a bigger monster than the criminals he was charged with apprehending.

He and Rachel had been married for ten years. She was a secretary at a prestigious law firm. Her boss, Joe Hayter, was working a capital murder case, and Ed was the lead detective. After a few dates, she moved in. They married and had a son, who is now six years old.

Carter and I pull up to a house on Wickard Drive, park, and get out. The neighborhood seems peaceful enough—manicured lawns, clean streets, trimmed bushes, and trees.

Knock, knock, knock. Carter knocks as my eyes scan over the property.

I'm not a realtor, but if I had to guess the value of the house, I'd say about three hundred grand. *I wonder what Rachel makes as a secretary.*

I knock on the door again. *Knock, knock, knock.* Still, no one comes. I check my watch. It's almost three in the afternoon.

"Do you think he's home? Maybe he has a side gig that's not on record," Carter says. He walks up to the front window, cups his face, and peers inside.

"He may just be out and about. I say we sit and wait, see if he pops back up," I suggest.

Carter agrees, and we head back to the car. Once the heater is on, I sit back and analyze the crime scene. My mind works through the progressions. I factor in all the evidence, trying to piece the puzzle together.

Suddenly, Carter's phone begins vibrating, interrupting my thought process.

"Hello," he answers. "Yeah, honey, I'm in the field right now. Um…" For some reason, he glances my way before answering. "I don't know. Hopefully not too late. Okay. Bye, babe. Love you."

He hangs up, puts the phone back in his pocket, turns to me, and says, "Liz said hi."

"Oh. Well, tell her I said hi," I reply with slight sourness. Don't get me wrong; Elizabeth isn't a bad person. She's never come at me sideways, despite the fact that she knows I spend more time with her husband than she does. I can respect that in a woman. She knows what she has and is confident in herself. Still, it doesn't change the fact that I want her husband in the worst way.

It's been a while since I've had someone between my legs, and my toys don't do the trick. Every day I'm around Carter, my juices bubble like a pot on the stove.

"I think that's him," Carter says, snapping me out of my fantasy.

A black Ford F-250 pulls into the driveway. Attached to it is a small fishing boat. We wait until the truck stops, and Edward Willis hops out. We approach him.

"Edward? Edward Willis?" I ask.

He turns and greets us with a warm smile. "Yes. How can I help you, officers?"

"Well, it's about your wife, Rachel. Can we come in?"

"Sure. Let me just grab the rest of my fishing gear."

Edward is a large man—six foot three, 240 pounds, skin the color of licorice, with a nice-sized *retirement* gut. Gray streaks run through his hair and beard. He walks with a slight limp due to an injury he took on the job some years back.

He reaches into the truck bed, grabbing his tackle box and a few fishing poles.

"I'll get that," I offer. "I know those tackle boxes are heavy as shit."

"Thank you for that, ma'am." He hands me the rods. I take a second to admire the craftsmanship. They look expensive as hell. I imagine myself on a boat in the middle of nowhere, trying to fish for bass. The way the poles are structured, it would be hard for me to work them properly.

As we step inside his home, he offers us drinks.

"No, thank you. We're on duty," I remind him.

He looks at me like I'm kidding. When he sees that I'm not, he pours himself a drink. "Okay. So what has my wife gotten herself into now?" he asks as he takes his first sip.

I look to Carter to lead. Maybe since they both belong to *The Guys* club, he'll receive the news better.

"Something has happened to your wife," Carter begins.

The way he says it gives Edward pause. I look for any signs of guilt.

His breathing becomes labored as his heartbeat quickens. "What has happened to my wife? Is she alright?"

"I'm sorry to tell you this, Mr. Willis, but your wife was murdered sometime last night or early this morning."

Edward's eyes get big. "What? What you mean, she got murdered? By who? Where?" His questions come sporadically. "Ohhh, nooo," he groans. "My son." Ed covers his face with his enormous left palm, trying to compose himself.

Carter gives him a moment to grieve before continuing. "You know this is all protocol, but we have to ask you some questions," Carter begins.

"Yes, of course. What do you need to know?"

"Well, let's start with your whereabouts. Where were you last night between the hours of 11 p.m. and 4 a.m.?"

"I was at a buddy of mine's lake house in Conroe."

"What's your friend's name?" I decide to chime in.

"Oh, you should know him. He still works for the department. Sam Anders." *Sam Anders?*

"Sam Anders? You're talking about the one who's head of Narcotics?" I ask.

"Yeah. That's my boy. We went to the academy together. He had a week off, so we decided to get some fishing in." *Well, there goes that lead.*

"Is there anything you can think of that may help us with this investigation?"

Ed tilts his head in contemplation. "I might. Hold on." He gets up and disappears toward the back of the house. A short time later, he reappears with a small, black journal in his left hand. Instead of handing it to Carter, he gives it to me. "This was her diary. She was always scribbling in it. Maybe she wrote something down that could help." I take it but don't dare look inside, not now. As an afterthought, Ed adds, "Rachel was sort of a perfectionist. She would often start on a page, then suddenly rip it out. I asked her why she always did that. She said she hated making mistakes."

"Well, thanks for the help, Mr. Willis," Carter says as we get up to leave.

"Please, call me Ed."

As we head for the door, my eyes sweep over a picture of Ed, Rachel, and their son, Ed Jr. It makes me pause. "Where's your son, Ed Jr.?"

"Oh, he's with his grandmother. He went to stay with her for Christmas break."

I stare at the boy with the curly afro and toffee-colored skin. *What a hell of a Christmas. Finding out your mom is dead, murdered, and you don't even know who did it.*

Carter and I make our exit. As soon as we step outside, it feels like the temperature has dropped at least ten degrees since we were in the house. We get in the car but don't speak, not until the heater kicks on, and our bones begin to defrost.

My partner turns to me and asks, "What do you think?"

I shrug. "Dead end. He was with Sam all week. Looks like he just got back into town."

"Just wanted to make sure we were on the same page."

I check the time. "How about we call it a night and start fresh in the morning? I know Liz wants you home A.S.A.P." I couldn't resist throwing that little barb in.

He chuckles but doesn't take the bait. "A'ight, I can go for that."

Carter puts the sedan in drive, and we head back to the precinct. I file and log the diary in the evidence locker, then head home.

There's something about this Willis case that's bothering the hell out of me. Once again, I let the evidence roll around in my head. I've learned that, sometimes, the biggest pieces of evidence are the ones we tend to overlook. Something is telling me this case is more than it appears. Whatever it is, I intend to find out.

Chapter 2

It's almost eleven o'clock at night when I pull into the driveway. Right now, I just need a nice, hot shower and a bottle of red wine. I grab my work bag and step into the cool, crisp night air. The chill soaks straight to my bones. I can't help but shiver as I close my car door.

"Heyyy, Unique!" I hear someone holler from behind me.

I turn around and spot my neighbors, Mr. and Mrs. Gaston. They look like they're heading out for the evening.

"Hey, y'all!"

Mrs. Gaston, or better yet, Daisy, is dressed in a slim-fitting black dress with matching heels. Draped over her shoulder is a cashmere coat to protect her from the elements.

Her husband, Art, is wearing black slacks and a black-and-white Armani dress shirt. Even though he's in his mid-forties, at six-two with a peanut-butter complexion, Art is still very much a dashing and attractive man.

They've been my neighbors for years now. Many nights, I've lain awake, fantasizing about Art having his way with me. I'm pretty confident I could have him if I tried, but a girl isn't trying to shit where she sleeps.

Art opens the door for his wife, then walks around to the driver's side. Before he gets in, we lock eyes. Then that knowing smile. *He knows he can have me if he wants.*

I feel my heart begin to quicken. I shake it off, turn, and head into my home. As soon as I step foot inside, I'm pissed. A pungent weed aroma assaults my senses. Out of my two kids, it could only be my son, Ka'Darious, who would try me like this.

Recently, I discovered he picked up the habit. Even though I don't approve, I'm not stupid enough to believe he'll stop just because I want him to, so I decided to let him smoke at the house, as long as it was in the backyard. I'd rather that than have him riding around, hotboxing with his friends, and risk getting pulled over. From what I'm smelling, he decided to disrespect me and smoke in the house anyway.

I sit my bag down by the couch and go searching for my troublesome fifteen-year-old. As I get closer to his bedroom door, I hear and feel the walls vibrating from his Bose stereo system. My hand grips the doorknob, but it won't turn. *He locked the door.*

Boom. Boom. Boom. "Ka'Darious, open the goddamn door!" I shout, pissed because I can't get to his ass.

Suddenly, the music stops. Muffled voices shift around inside. No doubt, he didn't expect me to be home early. I give him ten seconds to get his shit together before I beat on his door again.

Boom. Boom. Boom. "Ka'Darious, if you don't open this motherfu—"

The door swings open, and my red, glassy, slant-eyed son greets me in a pair of basketball shorts and a durag.

Looking at him, I'm astonished at how he's starting to look more and more like his daddy. He's already my height and will surely surpass me during his next growth spurt. "Wassup, Momma," this little negro has the nerve to say.

"Boy, don't *wassup* me. Why does my house smell like weed? What the hell did I tell your—" My voice catches in my throat when I spot someone else in the room. I check my watch. "Ka'Darious, what the hell is Steven doing over here this late? You know damn well I don't allow company after nine."

"But, Momma—" he tries.

"Don't *Momma* me. Steven, you need to get your things and go."

To be honest, I don't care much for Steven. Besides the fact that he's eighteen and far too old to be hanging around my son, Steven is also in a gang. Ever since they started hanging out, Ka'Darious hasn't wanted to wear anything blue, has become disrespectful, and I'm pretty sure Steven is the one who got my son smoking weed.

Even though he surpasses me in height, Steven walks past me with his head down. All I smell is weed as he slides by. I follow him to the front door and lock it behind him. *Now I need to set my son straight.*

When I walk back into his room, a sudden gust of cold air smacks me in the face. *His window's open.* I point toward it.

"It's too late for all that. Now you want to try to air this motherfucker out? Why would you disrespect me like that and smoke in my house when I specifically told you not to? I know you're going to smoke regardless, but I need you to do that shit outside, Ka'Darious."

He doesn't respond, but I need an answer. "Well?"

"Momma, we would've smoked outside, but it's cold as hell, and I didn't think you'd be back so soon." *Ain't this some shit?*

I can't even blame him for being honest. With no shirt on, it doesn't take long for him to start shivering. I shake my head and walk over to close his bedroom window. The detective in me scans his room for any other evidence of wrongdoing. Besides the sack of weed and blunt wraps on the dresser, I don't spot anything that raises alarms.

"And what did I tell you about company after nine o'clock?"

He sucks his teeth and looks away. One thing about my son, I can get on his ass all day, and he'll sit there and take it. The moment I start talking about one of his friends, he's quick to get defensive.

"You already know I don't like that boy, and you have him in my house past the deadline."

"A'ight, Momma. Next time, I'll just go to his house."

He knows I'm not going for that. Steven stays in a drug-infested, gang-riddled apartment complex, where homicides happen at least five or six times a year. Just the thought of my son hanging over there makes my skin crawl.

"No, you won't. If I even find out you're anywhere near there, I'll grab a couple guys from the precinct and roll up to get your ass. I know you won't like that."

He knows I'm not kidding. The worst thing you can be to those people in that complex is a cop or the son of a cop. If I show up with force, Ka'Darious won't be able to set foot in those projects again. But he may never forgive me. That's a card I'll only pull if I absolutely have to.

He shakes his head and bites his tongue. He's smart enough to know this is a battle he can't win. I don't want to pour it on him, so I turn and leave. Just before I step through the doorway, I turn back and ask, "Where's your sister?"

"I don't know," he says with a little too much bite.

I have a mind to get in his chest about it, but I let him have this one.

"Oh, Dad called," he adds.

That stops me dead in my tracks.

"What did he want?"

"To talk to you, but he said he wants us to come visit him this weekend."

My baby's daddy, Jessy, has been locked up for the last fourteen years. We've been together since high school, and even though our relationship has always been rocky, I truly love him.

When I turned eighteen, I got pregnant with Shantel. After having her, I made the decision to join the military, mostly for the benefits, but I also knew it would help when it came time to apply to the academy.

My mom, Gloria, was on drugs really badly and completely unfit to take care of a newborn baby girl. Surprisingly, Jessy stepped up. He quit the streets and got a job, doing whatever he could to take care of our daughter until I got back. Of course, I sent them money and visited whenever I could.

On one of my last visits home, I messed around and got pregnant again. It wasn't that big of a deal because I was due to be discharged a few months later. After four years of service, I came home and delivered my big-headed baby boy, Ka'Darious.

Everything was going well. We bought a house, and I applied to the academy. I was already told that, because of my service history, I was a shoo-in. Then everything came crashing down.

One night, Jessy and I were out on the town. By that time, Momma had finally gotten cleaned up. She'd been sober for two years. We felt comfortable leaving the kids in her care, so Jessy and I took a much-needed night out.

After we left the club, we searched for the car but realized we couldn't remember where it was parked.

"You know what, babe? Just wait here. I'll go find the car and pull back up on you," Jessy suggested.

It was a warm night, and I'd gotten a nice little buzz going, so I stood there, waiting for him to come back.

"Unique? I know that ain't your ass," a familiar voice called from behind me.

I turned around, and my heart dropped. My former sergeant, Sean Brown, was standing there, drunk and lit. He didn't look too happy to see me. I quickly scanned the parking lot, praying Jessy hadn't found the car yet.

Brown stalked toward me, his face set in a scowl. "So, this how you do a nigga, huh? You run home, then change your number?"

He looked at my stomach, about to ask something, then stopped himself.

Something behind me caught his eye. I turned my head to see Jessy pulling up.

"Please, Brown. Just leave me alone. We don't have anything to discuss, okay?" I turned and started walking away.

"Bitch. Where the fuck you think you're going?" he roared.

My steps quickened as I desperately tried to put space between us. He was right on my heels. The last thing I needed was a confrontation.

"You need to let me know what the fuck is going on."

He grabbed my arm. I instinctively turned around and smacked him in the face. His lip split and immediately began to bleed. Fury flashed in his eyes, and quick as a viper's strike, he backhanded me.

Whap.

I hit the ground, dirt smearing all over my dress.

"Bitch, have you lost your fucking mind, putting your hands on—"

I didn't even hear the car door open, but before Brown could finish his sentence, Jessy came across his face with the butt of my .45 Smith and Wesson.

Whap.

Instantly, his forehead split open. Blood dripped onto my dress as Brown collapsed and landed on top of me.

Jessy didn't stop there. Fueled by pure rage, he began beating Brown unmercifully.

Whap! Whap! Whap! Whap!

Blood sprayed onto me as I lay next to Brown in shock. A small part of me wanted him silenced, but suddenly, I realized he wasn't moving. Each blow Jessy rained down was met with a sick, wet thud. Brown didn't groan or yelp. Silent as a mime, his skull completely crushed.

I finally snapped, too. "Jessy! Jessy! Stop!"

Luckily, my voice cut through the chaos, and Jessy finally stopped his onslaught. Blood coated his arms. Splatters peppered his neck and face. The handle of my gun was slick with gore. In all that madness, we didn't notice a group of people standing nearby, watching in awe at the grotesque beating they'd just witnessed.

Suffice to say, the police were called, and Jessy went to jail for murder. Even though I swore to the police that Brown attacked me, the State wasn't trying to hear it. In their eyes, the beating was excessive.

They offered a plea deal of fifteen years, but Jessy took it to trial and lost. After being sentenced to fifty years, I was left to take care of the kids on my own.

Since I'm technically the reason he's locked up, I've been trying desperately to juggle being a mom, a prison wife, and a good officer of the law. And that shit is harder than it seems.

It's been a while since I took the kids to see their dad. Ka'Darious looks up at me expectantly. *This boy looks so much like his father.*

"If he calls back while I'm at work, let him know we'll be up there next weekend."

My son's smile lights up the room. "Bet. Thanks, Momma."

"Thank me for what? I'm supposed to take y'all to see your daddy. If I didn't, what kind of mother would I be?"

I close the door and head to my room for a shower. Passing my daughter's room, I decide to check on her.

Knock. Knock.

No answer.

I twist the knob and push the door open. Her room is neat and tidy but otherwise empty. She's nineteen, so I can't really be mad about her being gone. I told her that since she's in junior college, she doesn't have to work. I want her to focus on her studies. Instead, she uses her free time to hang with that no-good boyfriend of hers.

After closing her door, I head into my room and hop in the shower. As the water washes the day away, my thoughts drift back to Rachel Willis. I can't shake the image of her stabbed to death, lacerations across her neck and torso. Her unborn baby was robbed of a potentially great life.

Once I'm done, I lotion up, reach into my drawer, and grab my pink vibrator. Images of Art flash through my mind—him between my legs, sucking and slurping.

Then I picture myself bent over the arm of the sofa while Carter grips my hips, digging in my box. Before long, I'm cumming twice and drifting into sleep.

Beep. Beep. Beep.

I reach over and slap the snooze button on my clock. *Damn, four-thirty came fast.* It takes a few minutes to gather myself before I finally get up and start my day. A quick shower, a pot of coffee, and I'm out the door.

Imagine my surprise when I see my daughter walking in as I'm leaving. I make a show of checking the time. *4:45 a.m.*

She tries to slip past me, but I catch the scent of cigarette smoke and sex.

"I hope your ass is about to jump in the shower. A woman should never smell like that," I chastise her.

My daughter, Shantel, is the spitting image of me. At five-six, 142 pounds, she has a very curvaceous figure. Her breasts are C-cups, her waist is slim, and her hips are wide. I have no doubt that she's had her fair share of boys jumping in and out of her coochie. Her having sex is not what bothers me. It's her choice of men. Just like her momma used to do, Shantel is intent on dealing with dudes straight from the streets—the ones that only want to keep you around so they can brag about having a *bad bitch,* the ones that will eventually abandon you for another woman, a jail cell, or a grave plot. No matter how much I try to get her to see the light, my daughter is content with being blind.

She'll have to learn the hard way.

"Whatever, Momma. You're always trying to throw shade," this little heffa has the nerve to say. I fight the urge to snatch her up by her bundles.

"Throw shade? Girl, I don't have time to deal with your ass right now," I say as I continue out the door. As soon as I step outside, I spot her no-good, drug-dealing boyfriend, Mayo, parked in front of my house. I guess he's making sure she made it in safely.

You know I did my due diligence on him. Apparently, he's been to the county a few times for drug and weapons charges, but he hasn't done any serious time—yet. Both his parents are locked away on robbery charges, and his older sister was killed some time back.

He sees me about to get in my car and thinks it's a good idea to roll his window down and speak.

"How you doing, Ms. G?"

I snort, shake my head, and get in my car. Mayo pulls off, no doubt, feeling dejected. There's something about him that doesn't sit well with me. For his sake, I hope he does right by my daughter. If not, I'll be the one to take him down myself.

Chapter 3

I pull up to the precinct around 4:50 a.m. Technically, I'm over half an hour early, but I need to get a head start on this case. I notice Carter isn't here yet.

Probably had to break Liz off some before he left.

I scold myself for the thought. I have to get a grip on myself. Carter is a happily married man, and Liz and I are somewhat cool. What type of woman would I be if I push open that door?

The cold, morning air hits me like a shotgun blast. I fold within myself, pulling my coat even tighter around my body and scurrying off toward the entrance. I make it to the evidence room and check out Rachel Willis's diary. Once I get to my office, I fix myself another cup of coffee, sit down, and begin to comb through the pages.

The first couple of entries are pretty standard. She talks about her son, EJ, about her job and how she enjoys helping people, and then things get interesting. Apparently, her boss at the firm takes in a new client, a man named Gerald. Rachel appears to be smitten by him. She admits that he's a very "hardcore" individual but believes that's what turns her on. There's another entry where she states that she plans on meeting him for the first time.

My husband is going fishing this weekend. I told Gerald I want to spend the day together. Get to know him. He invited me to his neighborhood in Barrett Station. I've never been there, but I've heard it's a very dangerous place. He assures me that I will be safe. That turns me on.

I flip forward a couple of pages, but I notice some have been ripped out. Then suddenly, the pages have numbers instead of letters, arranged in some sort of pattern I'm unfamiliar with. *7E W368 T6 T43 M233.* What's odd is that not every page is written like this, but quite a few are. I scan through the rest of the book to see if I see Gerald being mentioned.

Nothing.

She talks about her husband, her kids, and her job. Oddly, there's no more mention of Gerald anywhere.

Maybe she got upset at him and ripped the pages out.

I sit the book down, allowing the problem to rotate in my head.

Knock, knock, knock.

I snap out of it.

Carter pokes his head into the room, holding up a bag of croissants. "Hungry?"

I can't help but smile. He knows I seldom eat before leaving for work in the morning. The aroma alone has my stomach growling.

"Starving," I reply as he steps in and takes a seat. I catch a whiff of his cologne, and it has my mouth watering.

"What you got going on?"

"Well, I was looking through her diary, and I think I found something interesting. It looks like our victim was stepping out on her husband."

Carter's eyebrows climb. "Really? Does it say with who?"

"Someone named Gerald. According to this, she met him at her job. He was one of her boss's clients. They met, and she fell hard."

"Does she mention anything that could've given him a motive?"

"That's the thing. I'm not sure. She goes from speaking highly of him to not mentioning him at all. At least, I don't think she does."

He frowns. "What do you mean you don't *think* she does?"

I grab a croissant from the bag and slide the diary over to him. Carter opens it and starts combing through the pages, just like I did. I watch his lips move as he reads. Confusion settles in when he reaches the coded pages, the same way it did for me.

"So that's why I said what I said. We need a way to crack the code. But first, we need to locate this Gerald character."

"Do we have a last name on him?"

"No, but I know who does. How do you feel about visiting our most beloved defense attorney?" I ask sarcastically.

"Well, I'll need to stop and get my hazmat suit."

"Come on, Carter. He's not that bad," I try to reason.

"Yeah, right."

I stuff the last bite of egg and cheese croissant into my mouth, stand up, and grab my coat. As we head toward the door, I look back at him. "You drove yesterday. Today, I'm driving."

On the way downtown, I spot a couple of teens standing on the corners, smoking weed, and obviously carrying concealed handguns. They look no older than Ka'Darious. I shake my head at the state the city has found itself in.

I remember when it was safe to play outside—building clubhouses in the nearby woods or going to the bayou and fishing for perch. Gangs have been around forever, but nowadays, it's different.

I can't count the times I've investigated a homicide, only to find out the perpetrator is barely old enough to drink. Back in my day, the gangsters were focused on getting money. They wanted to increase their dollar amount. These days, kids are worried about body counts. Then, when they get booked, they can't afford bonds or decent representation.

That's why I'm so hard on Ka'Darious. I know he's trying to find himself, and I worry he's looking for acceptance from the wrong crowd.

Then there's Shantel. I honestly don't know what to do with her. By all accounts, she's grown, and I know if I push too hard, she'll just use that as an excuse to leave. If she did, she'd move right in with that no-good boyfriend of hers. I hate to say it, but she reminds me of myself at her age.

Her daddy was knee-deep in the streets. If it weren't for my getting pregnant with her, he probably would've stayed there. The irony of it all is that he got out of the streets and still ended up with fifty years in the pen.

We exit off I-10 onto San Jacinto. I force myself to shake away thoughts of my family. When you're in the field, the slightest distraction can be your undoing. We cross over Fannin, heading south. It doesn't take long to reach our destination.

We arrive at the offices of the Marks and Bayter Law Firm. The suite sits on the twentieth floor of the building. As we step inside, it's clear the firm caters to high-end clients—granite walls, gold trimming, and Italian leather upholstery.

At the desk sits a young, Black woman with full, pouty lips, honey-brown skin, and a nice bubble butt.

"Excuse me." I flash my credentials. "We're here to see Mr. Bayter."

"Hold on a second." She picks up the receiver, dials an extension, has a brief conversation, then hangs up and leads us toward his office.

Joe Bayter is probably the department's most-hated defense attorney. In the eight years he's been practicing law, he hasn't lost a single case. When the State of Texas sees him across the aisle, knees buckle.

I'll admit, he's extremely handsome and an impeccable dresser. He notices us entering and stands to greet us.

"How can I help you—"

"Detectives," Carter cuts in for him. No doubt, he's ready to have a pissing contest with the slick, rich, successful defense attorney.

"Yes. Very well. How can I be of service, Detectives?"

"Well, we'd like to know about one of your former clients," I say.

Bayter tilts his head. "Whoa, whoa, whoa. I can't, under any circumstances, discuss my clients with you."

"Oh, no. We're not looking for that type of information. We just need a last name. First name, Gerald."

Joe studies us for a few heartbeats, then asks, "For what?"

"Sorry. Attorney-client privilege with the State of Texas," I shoot back.

He chuckles. "Only client I've had named Gerald was Gerald Blackwell."

I jot the name down in my notepad. "What can you tell us about Rachel?"

Joe's face sours at the mention of his former secretary. "Nothing much. Good clerical work, poor professionalism. Since you're asking about Blackwell, I assume you discovered they were fucking."

"So, this was common knowledge?" I ask, slightly surprised.

"Not really. I knew, but I'm not sure anyone else did. I told her that, while he was a client, she was strictly prohibited from dealing with him. She said she'd stop, but I highly doubted it."

"Would it be too much to ask for his address? We'll get it anyway. This would just save us a few minutes," I say.

Luckily, Joe gives us the address, and Carter and I head toward the Eastside.

When we pull into the community known as Barrett Station, it's obvious this isn't a place you want to be at night, especially alone. A well-known, gang-infested neighborhood, Barrett Station is home to the Crips. According to the file, Gerald is a known shot-caller.

"This the address right here," Carter says.

I park the sedan, and we both hop out. After checking our department-issued firearms, we approach the door of a small, blue-and-white house.

Knock, knock, knock.

"Who is it?" a woman yells from what sounds like the back of the house.

"Police!" I call out.

No response. I'm pretty sure she's taking her time to alert whoever's inside and hide whatever contraband she can. Nearly two minutes later, the door finally swings open.

A bright-skinned woman with blue weave, denim shorts, and a British Knights tee stands in the doorway. "Can I help you?"

"Yes. I'm Detective Gordon, and this is Detective Carter. We're here to speak with Gerald Blackwell. We have reason to believe he resides here."

Her eyes dart away as she considers lying. Wisely, she decides against it.

"Hold on. G-Baby! They got some laws out here tryna talk to you!" she yells toward the back of the house.

"He's coming," she says, turning and walking back inside.

Moments later, Gerald "G-Baby" Blackwell appears. I'll be honest; the man has my kitty purring. He stood six-foot-two, 220 pounds, skin the color of Dutch chocolate. With no shirt on, I get a full look at his collection of tattoos.

A lot of the tattoos are gang-related, but some are portraits of loved ones. Others depict symbols that represent Texas, like highways, sports teams, and things like that. I can't resist checking out his print. *The man definitely looks like he's packing something.*

"How you doing, Gerald? I'm Detective Carter. We want to speak to you about Rachel Willis."

Gerald flinches, just slightly, but recovers quickly. "Who? I don't know any Rachel."

Carter looks at me, confused. For a brief moment, we actually consider that we may have the wrong guy. But something tells me he's lying. *But why?*

"Well, Gerald, we have evidence showing otherwise."

"Look, I don't care what your evidence shows. I'm telling you, I don't know any Rachel," he argues.

"Well, Rachel was found murdered yesterday morning," I say.

He can't hide the reaction, even if he wants to. His face falls, the bravado he showed earlier evaporating instantly. Carter notices it too and looks at me before I continue.

"We just need to ask you some questions—"

"Look, Detective. I don't know shit. I don't know any Rachel, and I damn sure don't know about any murder. I'm not tryna waste either of our time by giving you answers I don't have."

"Well, we—"

Slam.

He shuts the door in my face.

I swallow back my anger. You'd think if he shared any kind of emotional bond with Rachel Willis, he'd want to help solve her murder. *Unless he's the murderer.*

I close my eyes and count to ten before turning around and heading back to the car.

As we get in and shut the doors, I notice people stepping out of their homes, dressed in blue with matching bandanas. They begin to converge on us.

We're in an unmarked car, wearing plain clothes. They could easily claim they didn't know we were police. At first, it looks like only a few. Then the few become many. Even though no weapons are visible, I'd bet my badge that most of them are strapped.

I turn the engine over, but now they're blocking my path.

"Fuck this," Carter mutters, grabbing the door handle. He already has his Glock out, ready.

"No, Carter," I blurt, grabbing his hand. "Don't step out with your pistol. These dudes won't hesitate to shoot. Let me handle it."

He looks unsure but decides to trust me. This is my arena. Carter grew up in the suburbs. I'm a hood, project chick, through and through.

I kill the ignition and open my driver-side door. I hold my hands out to show I'm unarmed.

"I'm Detective Gordon, and this is my partner, Detective Carter. I know y'all didn't realize we were police, but"—I flip out my credentials—"y'all know now, so I suggest you clear a path so we can leave."

The crowd goes quiet. A lot of them look toward the big homies, waiting for direction. Finally, a dark-skinned man with a glass eye and a scar across his cheek speaks up.

"Let them go."

Just like that, the crowd parts down the middle, giving us a clear path out of the neighborhood.

I crank the engine, press the gas, and get the hell out of dodge.

A couple of days later, I'm sitting at my desk, still trying to make sense of the coded passages in Rachel's diary. The other pages haven't offered much help. Something keeps telling me the key to this case is buried in that code.

Knock, knock.

Carter pokes his head in. "Wassup?"

"Forensics just got back," he says. "They sent an email. Check it out."

I log into my account. The DNA analysis on the hat and the knife has come in. They were cross-examined against Gerald's DNA. My jaw drops when I see the results. Both came back a match. *Got ya.*

Carter, having already read it, grins. "He don't know her, my ass."

I stand and grab my coat.

"Judge Wiseman's already drawing up the warrant," Carter says as we head out the door.

I turn back to him. “Get the team together. I don’t want to pull up on him with anything less than twenty, armed and ready.”

“Certainly.”

We head downstairs and link up with the tactical team, along with the Gulf Coast Task Force. We suit up and prepare to serve a very high-risk warrant.

It’s 4:15 a.m. The team makes our final assembly at the carwash down the street from Gerald’s home. I strap on my vest, making sure my Glock is loaded and ready.

The streets are virtually deserted. Hopefully, we catch him asleep so he won’t put up much of a fight. Worst-case scenario, he’s got a house full of gang members with fully loaded weapons. I whisper a quick prayer that I’ll make it back to my kids.

The team lead, Sergeant Ritter, gives the signal to move out. Moments later, we’re parked on G-Baby’s street. Carter and I hop out, badges swinging from our necks, pistols at our sides.

We’re positioned at the front and back doors, one officer on each side, battering ram in the middle. Ritter knocks twice, softly.

Knock, knock.

Before anyone can respond, the ram slams forward.

Boom.

The door caves in.

“Police! Police! U.S. Marshals! Everybody on the ground!”

We fan out through the small house. The living room and kitchen are empty. We find G-Baby in the bedroom, he and his girlfriend, Tierra, asleep in bed, both naked.

G-Baby jolts awake and looks like he’s about to reach for something, then thinks better of it. Once he realizes we’re law enforcement and not jackers, he resigns himself, lowers his head, and sighs.

I step up as he sits on the edge of the bed, his semi-hard cock hanging over the side.

"Gerald Blackwell, you're being charged with the murder of Rachel Willis and her unborn child, Baby John Doe. You have the right to remain silent. Anything—"

Tierra starts screaming. "Nooo! Get the fuck outta my house! Get the fuck out!"

One of the officers restrains her, threatening detainment if she doesn't calm down.

"Get him some clothes!" I shout.

Another officer hands over a pair of boxer briefs, basketball shorts, and an old pair of blue-and-white Air Jordans. Gerald slips them on, and we escort him out.

It doesn't take long for the neighborhood to figure out what's happening. By the time we walk Gerald to the squad car, the street is flooded with blue. Officers push the crowd back as we move him through.

"Hold your head up, cuz!" someone yells.

Gerald nods, then ducks his head as we seat him in the back.

"I thought you said you didn't know Rachel," I say later, sitting across from him in the interrogation room.

He keeps his head down, probably trying to figure out how we caught up to him. *Because you dropped the murder weapon, you idiot.*

Normally, I wouldn't waste time interviewing someone when I've got a smoking gun, but there's something about this case that keeps clawing at the back of my mind. Everything feels too convenient.

"This is your chance to help yourself. Maybe if you confess, the State will give you something you can work with. I'll be honest, they're already talking about upgrading this to a capital case. I'm pretty sure they'll seek the death penalty. You killed an unborn baby, after all."

"I ain't killed no one," he finally blurts.

I let out a small laugh. "That's funny. We found your DNA on the knife used to kill her. Your DNA was also on a hat found at the scene. Add that to the fact you claimed you didn't even know her—"

"Because Tierra was there. I didn't want her to know I…" His voice cracks.

"You didn't want her to know what? That you were fucking the white, law firm secretary?"

Gerald shakes his head like he can make the problem disappear. He closes his eyes, tilts his head back, holds it there for a moment, then drops it again. When he opens his eyes, they lock onto mine.

"Look. I met Rachel when I was fighting a manslaughter charge. She was my lawyer's secretary. One day, when I went up there to make a payment, we met and clicked. Both of us were dealing with someone, so we agreed to keep things discreet. Six months after we started messing around, she told me she was pregnant. I really wasn't feeling that, but she made it clear she wasn't getting rid of the baby."

He pauses, thinking, then lets out a gruff laugh. "She said her husband was Black, so if I didn't want to play daddy, she could put it off on him. The last time I saw her was about a week ago. She pulled up, tryna spend some time. Said her husband had gone out of town, fishing. I fucked her down, let her suck my dick, then sent her on her way. On the set, she was alive when she left."

"So, what about the knife? Why were your prints all over it?" I ask.

"I gave her that knife for protection. She didn't want to deal with having a gun, so I made her carry a blade. I had just given it to her that night."

Gerald's eyes plead with me to believe him. The crazy thing is, I kind of do. G-Baby is a career criminal who knows better than to leave a murder weapon at the scene. Everything feels too convenient for my taste. Of course, I don't let him know that.

There's nothing I can do about the charge. He still has to go through the process. So instead, I play hardball.

"Well, maybe if you would've given us this information earlier, you could've helped yourself. Now you'll need to hire a lawyer to help you."

I stand up, leaving Gerald alone to stew. When I approach Carter, he's still watching Gerald on the monitor.

"What do you think?" I ask.

"I think he's full of shit. If that were true, he could've told us that from the jump. Sounds like he spent the ride over here coming up with a convenient story," Carter says.

"That's the thing. I think he's telling the truth. Gerald's seasoned. One of the cardinal rules is you don't leave the murder weapon behind. He knows that. Even if he somehow did, he's smart enough to admit knowing her. He could've easily told us the same story from the beginning. Why lie if you know we have the knife? Obviously, he didn't know it was used in the killing. And if he didn't know that, then he couldn't have committed the crime."

Carter sighs. "Okay, maybe he didn't do it himself, but what if he had someone else do it? Maybe that person used the knife and didn't tell Gerald out of fear. Maybe he had one of his Crip homeboys kill her and the baby as retaliation for not getting the abortion."

I nod. "That's definitely possible."

Then something clicks.

I grab a pen and a sheet of paper and take it back into the room. Gerald looks confused when he sees me, probably thinking I'm fishing for a confession.

"I want you to write down exactly what you just told me," I say.

He takes the pen and paper and starts writing. I step back out of the room.

"What was that about?" Carter asks as we watch Gerald through the glass.

"The Medical Examiner said the wounds were consistent with a left-handed swing," I say quietly.

Carter's eyes widen. "Gerald's right-handed."

"Exactly. That tells us he didn't wield the knife himself."

We notify transport that we're done with the suspect, and Gerald is taken to Harris County Jail to be booked.

I sit in my office, going over everything we've learned so far. *If Gerald didn't do it, and the husband was out of town, then who killed Rachel Willis?*

Even with someone in custody, I don't feel any closer to the truth.

My phone vibrates. It's a text from Ka'Darious.

Don't 4get. Gotta go zee dad 2morrow.

I reply, *Finishing up now. OTW home.*

I tuck my phone into my purse, clean off my desk, and head home for the night.

Chapter 4

As we pull up to the Stiles Unit in Beaumont, Texas, my nerves become frayed. I absolutely despise coming to the prison, but I have no choice. It's my duty to make sure my kids know who their father is. After we get searched and hit with the K-9 dogs, we make our way to the front desk.

"I'm here to see Jessy Frazier," I tell the dark-skinned officer manning the desk. She looks to be in her mid-to-late twenties. Her hair is styled in braids, her nails short but painted white. I notice a slight twitch in her face when I say my baby daddy's name.

"Who?" she asks with a bit of attitude.

"Frazier. Jessy Frazier."

"Okay, fill this out," she says, eyeing my kids suspiciously.

Jessy must be fucking this bitch. I can't help the pang of jealousy that hits me, knowing another woman might be getting what I can't.

After filling out the slip, the kids and I head to the visitation room. The detective in me surveys the surroundings. The room is packed with women and children. I can't help but wonder if the women's prison looks the same. *Probably not.*

I spot an interracial couple—a beautiful, White brunette chatting it up with a Black man who looks like he's straight out of the projects. Rachel Willis crosses my mind. She apparently had a thing for Black men, dangerous ones at that.

Finally, they escort Jessy into the visitation room. His clothes are pressed, and his haircut is pristine. That's one thing I can say. No matter what, he always looks his best.

Both my son and daughter tense up at the sight of their dad. At five-ten and 180 pounds, Jessy isn't an imposing figure. His laid-back, disarming demeanor might make you think he's friendly. But Jessy has a quick, deadly temper, one that's gotten him into trouble more than once. Even though I'm an officer of the law, there's something about my baby daddy that still gives me chills.

As he approaches the table, the kids jump up to greet him. "Heyy, Dad!" they sing in unison as he pulls them into a big hug.

"What's up, y'all? Both of y'all done got big as hell on me." He looks at Ka'Darious. "You look just like your momma."

"I think he looks like you," I say, slightly irritated that he hasn't acknowledged me yet.

He catches my tone, turns, and finally greets me. "What's up, Uniquha?" He's the only one besides my momma who still calls me by my real name. He pulls me in for a hug, and I let him.

Wrapped in his arms, I let the stress of life melt away for just a moment. I have no doubt that if he weren't locked up, Jessy and I would be married.

"Nothing much. How you been?" I ask.

"Same old shit. Doing time."

"Did you go to store?" I ask.

"Yeah, the money was down there. Appreciate it," he says. I can tell he's itching to talk to me about something, but he's a good enough dad to focus on the kids first.

For the first hour and a half, we talk about them—school, friends, and how they've been doing. I feel a twinge of jealousy at how comfortable they are with him. With me, they're guarded. I can barely get a conversation out of them without it turning into an argument.

When Jessy sees the time winding down, he turns to Shantel. "Shay, can you do me a favor? I'm tryna holla at your momma about something real quick."

"Sure thing, Dad." She grabs Ka'Darious, and they head toward the vending machines.

I take a deep breath and brace myself. I already know what this is about, and I really don't want to hear it. Still, he leans in.

"Goddamn, U, why you ain't answer the phone when I had ole girl call?" he asks in a harsh whisper.

Ole girl. He's talking about some CO he convinced to help him hustle drugs inside the penitentiary. This negro really wants me, a homicide detective, to help facilitate smuggling contraband into a penal institution.

"I told you, Jessy. I'm not about to get caught up helping you bring drugs in—"

"It's not drugs!" he almost shouts. He looks around, then lowers his head and his voice. "It's tobacco, U. You act like a nigga want you handling meth or some shit."

"I don't give a damn if it's bubblegum. I'm not doing that shit." I love my baby daddy, and he made the ultimate sacrifice for me, but I have to draw the line somewhere.

His jaw clenches. He wants to explode, but he uses every ounce of self-control to hold it in. "Okay, then why you ain't send her the money?"

"I'm not doing that either. They can trace that shit. Jessy, you act like I'm not out here taking care of your kids. You act like—"

"Bitch, you act like I'm not in this motherfucker behind you," he growls through clenched teeth. *There it is.* He always throws that in my face. "I don't ask for much. And the little shit I do ask for, you act like you can't make the smallest sacrifice."

"I don't know why you feel like you have to hustle," I say. "I make sure you've got money on your books and on e-comms. You're not in here hurting for anything." For the life of me, I can't understand why this man feels the need to put himself, or me, at risk. In fourteen-plus years, he's never missed store.

"You think I like depending on my bitch?" he seethes.

I flinch at the word. Even though we're not technically together, I still want him to call me something soft.

"What happens when you decide to up and leave? When some other nigga comes along and has you dizzy off the dick? All of a sudden, you don't want to be a prison wife anymore. Then what?"

I know he's afraid I'll leave. I get that. But if I were going to walk away, I would've done it in year one. I damn sure wouldn't have spent thousands of dollars taking care of him.

"Jessy, I know the sacrifice you made for me, and I will always appreciate and love you for that. There's not a man on this earth with dick good enough to make me forsake my duty as a real woman. I got you. I will continue to hold you down, but I can't risk myself like that. If something goes wrong, then I'm no good to you or the kids. I need you to understand that."

"Oh, I see what it is. You want a nigga on a leash. As long as I depend on you, you in control."

I jerk back like I've been slapped. "Are you serious?" Now this motherfucker has me all the way turned. I have half a mind to slap the shit out of him, but instead, I keep it classy. "You know what, Jessy? Get at me when you get your mind right."

I stand just as the kids are walking back to the table. "Kids, say goodbye to your dad."

I walk off and don't look back until I'm outside. I'm so upset that my hands won't stop trembling.

He knows I feel guilty about what happened. That night still haunts me. Jessy did what he did because he believed he was protecting me. Afterward, I told him I didn't know the man he beat to death in the club parking lot, when in fact, I knew him very well.

September 2007.

I had just completed basic training and officially became a member of the U.S. Army. I honestly didn't think I'd make it through. My whole life, I'd never really done anything physically demanding. When basic training was first mentioned, I was sure I would fail. Not only did I pass, but I did it with exemplary marks.

My girl Sanders and I were sitting in the DFAC, grabbing chow. Something caught her attention. Without saying a word, she got up and walked over. I followed her path, and my eyes landed on our staff sergeant, Brown.

Staff Sergeant Brown had a reputation as a hard-nosed superior officer. With me, though, he'd always been pleasant. At five foot eleven, 190 pounds, his arms, chest, and stomach were chiseled. The man was built like a machine.

He had smooth, chocolate skin with a set of full lips. He had plenty of us women creaming on ourselves whenever he came around.

At first, I thought he was about to chew her out about something, but suddenly, she turned and headed my way, a big Kool-Aid smile on her lips.

"Girrrll, you not finna believe this," she drawled.

Sanders was from Houston, Dead End, and one of the only females I could truly relate to. She stood about five-three, 125 pounds, with a slim-thick frame. We'd been rocking since we did our physicals together.

"Girl, what?"

"Sergeant Brown wants to talk to you. He said, since we've completed basic training, he wants to take you out on a date."

I almost laughed. What kind of man is scared to come holla at a woman he wants?

"You know I got a man at home," I told her, hoping that'd be enough to make her drop it.

"So? He ain't asking you to suck his dick. He just wants to go on a date. You need a little fun. Play dress-up. Let your hair down," she pressed.

I glanced over at Sergeant Brown as he stood there, looking all shy and shit.

Fuck it. Why not? It's just a date.

Present Day

"Hey, Momma, can we grab some boudin balls on the way home?" Ka'Darious asks as they step out of the prison and meet me on the walkway.

"Sure. Where you want them from?"

"Bonfire," he and Shantel say at the same time.

I smile. "Y'all have a good time?"

"Yeah. When are we coming back?" Ka'Darious asks, hopeful.

"I don't know yet, but it won't be too long from now," I promise as we get in the car and make the hour-long drive home.

No matter how upset I am with Jessy, I'll never stop the kids from seeing him. I grew up without my dad and refuse to let them experience that.

***

"What are you trying to tell me, Rachel Willis?" I mumble as I sit at my desk, staring at the crime-scene photos.

It's been two and a half weeks since we arrested and indicted Gerald Blackwell for the murders of Rachel and her unborn child, but I'm no closer to easing the uneasiness gnawing at me. Without an alternate suspect, I can't go to the higher-ups and argue that we've got the wrong man.

Knock, knock, knock.

"Come in."

Lieutenant Anders pokes his head into my office. After Ed Willis gave us his alleged whereabouts for the night in question, we double-checked with Lt. Anders, and he confirmed the alibi. Since then, we haven't spoken. He's Narcotics, and I'm Homicide. Our paths rarely cross, yet here he is.

"Hey, Lieutenant. What's going on?"

He steps inside, wearing a plain blue dress shirt and khaki slacks. A middle-aged white man with a bald head and a slight gut, Lt. Anders gives off the impression of a good-ole-boy redneck.

In reality, he has a Black wife and four biracial kids at home.

"What's going on, Gordon?" he asks.

It doesn't go unnoticed how he tries to sneak a look at what I've been working on. I casually cover the file with my forearm, lean against the desk, and ask, "How can I help you?"

"I just wanted to stop by and see how things were going. I've heard a rumor that you're considering dismissing Gerald Blackwell as the primary suspect."

Who the hell told him that?

Only two people know: my partner and my lieutenant in homicide.

"Well, I wouldn't say I'm dismissing him. I'm just open to exploring other possibilities."

He doesn't look pleased, so I call it out. "Is there something wrong with that? You're in Narcotics, and I don't see how this affects any case you're working."

"No, no, it doesn't," he says. "To be honest, Rachel and I were good friends. Ed and I have been close for almost thirty years. Rachel and my wife used to go out together. Their son and my kids go to the same school, sleepovers and all that. I just don't want to see her swept under the rug because of bureaucratic bullshit."

"Well, I can understand and respect that you have a personal interest in solving her murder. As do I. But I also have a duty to make sure we have the right person responsible. Right now, everything *looks* like it points to

Gerald Blackwell, but I want to cross all my T's and dot all my I's."

Lieutenant Anders nods slowly, like I'm making perfect sense. "Well, I'll let you carry on then."

"Okay. Thank you."

He heads out, and I get back to work. *Blackwell.*

If Rachel and Gerald were as close as I suspect, then it's highly likely the child was his. And if that's true, it stands to reason he may have known about her diary. An idea hits me. I grab my coat, slip the diary into my bag, and head for the door.

Carter notices me and lifts his hands, palms up. *What's up?* He wants to know what happened with the lieutenant and if I need backup. I shake my head, letting him know I've got this one.

As I step outside and head toward my car, an eerie feeling crawls up my spine, like I'm being watched. I scan the area, my heart thudding heavily in my chest. *Thump. Thump. Thump.*

I slow my breathing and focus on my surroundings. Wind howls, licking against my face. Even though it's midmorning, the sun is hidden behind dark clouds, casting everything in shadow.

After a few seconds of paranoia, I shake it off and climb into my vehicle, heading downtown to the Harris County Jail.

It doesn't take long for them to bring Gerald "G-Baby" Blackwell out. He's handcuffed and shackled, but he still carries a commanding presence.

His file paints him as a ruthless general overseeing more than thirty Crip members, arrests ranging from manslaughter to weapons charges, and now capital murder. G-Baby is a seasoned criminal, as tough as they come.

But now, he looks broken. He's lost at least ten pounds since being locked up. Dark bags sit under his eyes. The

State has officially decided to pursue the death penalty. When he spots me, something flickers in his eyes. *Hope.*

"Gerald, how are you doing?" I ask.

"Well, considering, not too good. These bitch-ass officers keep fucking with me, calling me baby killer, jacking me for my food, and—" He stops himself, remembering he's venting to a cop, not family. "What's up? Why you here?" he asks.

"I've been doing a lot of thinking, and I'm starting to believe your story."

He sits up straighter. *Now I've got his attention.*

"A lot of the evidence was too conveniently left at the scene. I know you've been doing this long enough not to make rookie mistakes. It's possible you're innocent."

His shoulders drop with relief.

"But," I add, taking the wind out of his sails, "until I can prove it, I'm just one detective with a hunch. All the evidence still points to you, and the State won't drop the charges unless I bring them another suspect."

"So, what does that mean?" he asks.

"It means I need your help. I know how you feel about helping the police, but if you don't, you could be convicted and sentenced to death." I pause and let that sink in.

Gerald closes his eyes, thinking. When he opens them, there's something different there. Resolve. "Okay," he says. "What you need me to do?"

"What do you know about Rachel's diary?"

"She told me she kept one. But what about it?"

"The diary is how we found out about you. She—"

"How did you crack the code?" he cuts in.

Now it's my turn to sit up straight. "What do you know about the code?"

"Everything," he says calmly. "I'm the one who gave it to her."

My heart jumps into my throat. The whole time, the answers were sitting right in front of me.

I pull the diary from my bag and place it on the table between us.

"So, you're the one who taught her the code?"

"Yeah. She told me she'd been keeping a diary, but she felt her husband had found it and was reading it. She hid it, but she was always paranoid about him finding it again. So, I told her to write everything in code."

His explanation is so simple that I almost laugh.

"Well, I really need the code so I can decipher what's in the book. Can you do that for me?"

"Sure. If it's gonna help prove my innocence, then hell yeah."

I pull out a pad and pen and watch as G-Baby breaks down a simple yet elegant coding system. By the time we finish, my entire body is buzzing with excitement. *Finally, a real step toward finding the true killer of Rachel Willis.*

I head home from the precinct with the diary tucked deep in my bag. Even though we're not supposed to transport or remove evidence, I know I won't sleep until I've studied and cracked the code.

As I exit the freeway, I check my rearview mirror before merging into the left lane.

What the hell?

I might be tripping, but the same pair of headlights has been following me since I left the county jail. I make a left under the freeway. Sure enough, the car turns with me. Whoever it is knows how to keep their distance, always leaving at least one car between us. If it weren't for my training, I probably wouldn't have noticed.

Now that we're in a residential area, I'm slowed down by streetlights and stop signs. I ease my hand into my bag, grip my Sig, and rest it on my lap. I don't want to jump the gun. This could be paranoia. But I also don't want to lead them straight to my house. I turn into a neighborhood I know well.

Simmeron.

Almost immediately, I realize my mistake. Too many of the streetlights have been shot out. With barely any visibility, if something were to go down, the chances of finding a credible witness would be slim to none.

The car behind me turns.

Now it's just me and my pursuer.

I make a quick right down a side street. The car follows.

Okay. This ain't coincidence.

I debate calling for backup, but something stops me. Instead, a different instinct kicks in. I know there's a dead end coming up. I mash the gas, gain about thirty yards, then make a sharp left.

As soon as I turn, I stop, park, and hop out. My pistol is loaded, up and ready. Whoever comes around that corner is about to meet an angry Black woman with a gun.

It's cold, but my blood is rushing like rapids. Headlights appear, reflecting off the pavement. I steady myself. As soon as the vehicle turns, my pistol will be aimed at the driver's side window.

Rrrrhh.

The vehicle swerves and comes to a hard stop.

What the fuck? A van?

The occupants throw their hands up, begging me not to shoot. That's when it hits me. This isn't the car that followed me. That was a sedan, not a van.

Was I tripping?

Now I'm thinking I imagined the whole thing. I show the people in the van my credentials, assure them they're not about to die, then hop back in my car and head home. The entire drive, my hands won't stop trembling.

As soon as I get inside, I pour myself a stiff drink. Ka'Darious is in his room, playing online, and Shantel is gone again. The shower is hot and soothing. I shudder at how close I came to killing innocent people.

Get a grip on yourself, Uniquha.

I step out of the shower and throw on purple boxer shorts, a sports bra, and a kimono robe. I double-check the locks on all the doors and windows before sitting at my desk.

I flip to the first coded page in the diary, then pull out the key Blackwell gave me. It looks simple enough, but translating each letter proves tedious. The first coded entry reads:

2P74L 4

8032Y 9A7 2 B1A8T4F8L 32Y

After several minutes of work, it finally comes together:

April 4

Today was a beautiful day.

I spend the next couple of hours decoding Rachel's most intimate thoughts. When I finish, I reread the entries and feel my stomach drop. Apparently, Rachel had a run-in with one of Gerald's relatives—his younger brother, Cam. From the looks of it, the encounter did not go well at all.

I never meet up with Gerald at his house, because his girlfriend lives there. We use different locations for our rendezvous. Today, we were supposed to meet at his brother Cam's apartment on the north side.

When I arrived, I noticed Gerald's car was gone. I knocked and learned he had stepped out on a run and would be back shortly. I decided to wait. His brother had always been nice to me, so I figured it wouldn't be a problem.

"You want something to drink?" Cam offered.

Something told me I shouldn't have, but I accepted. Once I sat down, Cam started going on and on about how pretty I was and how lucky his brother was to have such a beautiful, white woman on his arm. I started feeling uncomfortable but didn't want to leave. I needed to see Gerald, and I was willing to wait.

Suddenly, the liquor began to take a serious effect on me. My eyelids grew heavy, and before I knew it, I must have passed out.

When I came to, I was alone on the couch with only my shirt on. My shorts were on the floor beside me, and my panties had been pushed aside.

I frantically searched for my things and called Gerald. He answered immediately. Imagine my surprise when he told me he was out of town and had asked his brother to let me know he wouldn't be back for a few days. Apparently, his phone wasn't getting good service where he was.

I felt sick to my stomach and thought I was going to throw up. I wanted to tell Gerald what his brother had done to me, but I was terrified of his reaction. Gerald is a very dangerous man, but so is his little brother. I don't want to be the reason they get into it, and something happens that I'd regret.

After hanging up, I stepped outside and saw Cam standing by a car with a group of his friends. I froze, unsure what to say or do. When they noticed me, the smirks on their faces made me feel dirty and ashamed.

That shame turned into anger. The anger turned into rage. Then I exploded. After calling him a sick, perverted rapist, I jumped in my car and sped off. I was so hurt that I had to pull over just to cry.

I know I should call the police. If I do, Gerald will never forgive me for sending his little brother to jail. Then I would have to explain to my husband why I was at Cam's apartment in the first place. What should I do?

After double-checking my translation, I read the entry again. Then again. I log onto my computer and type in *Cameron Blackwell.*

At twenty-five years old, he's no stranger to the criminal justice system. He's done a few state jail stints for manufacturing and delivering, along with weapons charges.

Just like his older brother, he's an avid and active member of the Crips. I call in a favor and get his home address. I glance at the clock. *11:15 p.m.*

I know I shouldn't do this. It goes against protocol. Still, I throw on some clothes, grab my jacket, strap my Sig, and head out the door.

I pull up to the Sterling Shire Apartments on Mesa Road. Gang members are outside, smoking cigarettes, weed, and K-2 mixed with wet. I'm in my personal vehicle, dressed as a civilian, so I have to move carefully.

After locating his apartment number, I park and hop out, my gun tucked into the small of my back. I walk up to the door.

Knock, knock, knock.

No answer.

I check my watch, then knock again.

Knock, knock, knock.

Just as I'm about to lose patience and leave, the locks click, and the knob turns. Standing there in nothing but blue basketball shorts, no drawers, as if he threw them on in a rush, is Cameron Blackwell.

"How are you doing, Mr. Blackwell? I'm Detective Gordon with the Harris County Sheriff's Department. I need to speak with you about a recent incident."

He looks behind him, then left to right. "You by yourself?" It sounds more like an accusation than a question.

"Well, I figured I'd come like this so if you decided to talk to me, nobody could spread rumors that you were speaking to the police." He smiles at that. The fact that I considered his reputation clearly appeals to him.

"What incident you talking about?"

"Well, it's cold as hell out here. I was hoping we could discuss that inside."

"Oh yeah, my bad. Come in."

I step inside and take a quick look around his apartment. It's pretty bare, a couple of leather sofas and a sixty-inch TV.

I notice the bedroom door is open. What looks like a woman is stretched out on the bed. I can only see her from the knee down. There's a rose tattoo on her right calf. I take a seat on the couch while Cam closes the bedroom door. When he comes back, he sits across from me, legs spread wide. I resist the urge to look at his crotch.

"So, what's up, Detective? To what do I owe the pleasure?"

My mind flashes back to Rachel's diary. "Do you happen to know a woman by the name of Rachel Willis?"

His face hardens. The friendly demeanor he had earlier disappears. "Yeah, I know her," he spits. "What about her?"

"I'm sure you know she's dead. Murdered. Her and her unborn child. I recently located a diary that mentions you."

He leans back, instantly defensive. "Mentions me? How?"

"She claims she came to see your brother, but you lied about his whereabouts. While she waited, you offered her a drink. After consuming it, she passed out. When she woke up, her clothes were missing, and she believed she'd been raped."

"Rape?" Cam's face twists with anger. "Ain't nobody raped that bitch," he snaps.

"I didn't say you did. That's why I'm here. To hear your side of the story."

Cam exhales, shakes his head, and starts talking. "I told my brother she wasn't shit. He never listens. She came over, looking for him. I told her he was gone and wouldn't be back anytime soon. She said she talked to him and that he told her he would. Neither of us could call him because his phone wasn't working. I didn't care if she waited. She asked if I had something to drink. I offered her a Coke. She wanted something stronger, so I poured her a glass of Hennessy.

"A few of my homies were supposed to stop by so we could discuss some business. Of course, when they saw a White girl in my living room, they started shooting their shot. About ten minutes later, my phone rang. I stepped outside to take the call. I was gone less than twenty minutes. When I came back in, Rachel was getting handled by two of my homies, one from behind, the other in her face. My jaw dropped. No cap, I joined in where I could. We spent the next hour wearing her out until she passed out on the couch. Later, we were all outside, chilling. She came out, talking about rape and all kinds of other shit."

As Cam tells his story, I watch him closely for any signs of deception: nervous tics, shifting eyes, anything. *I don't see it.*

Either he's telling the truth, or he's an exceptional liar. I still need to figure out which hand he favors.

Suddenly, there's an aggressive knock at the door.

Boom, boom, boom!

Cam looks at me like I set him up, and the SWAT team is about to storm his place.

I shrug. *Your guess is as good as mine.*

He opens the door, and three of his homies rush inside.

"Cuz, we got a problem. Pookie just hit us. The lick they went—"

Cam cuts him off. "This ain't the time. Wait outside. I'm about to get dressed, then we'll talk."

The guy looks like he wants to keep going, but one look from Cam shuts him down completely.

They all look at me. *This is my cue.*

"A'ight, Cam, I'll catch up with you later," I say, making a move to leave.

The other two don't know I'm a detective, and I'm pretty sure Cam wants to keep it that way. As I pass him, Cam pulls me into a hug, making sure to palm my ass in the process.

"What the hell are you doing?" I whisper.

"A'ight, Tay," he says loudly for their benefit, then lets me go.

I want to punch him in his face for trying me, but if looks could kill, Cam would be laid out with a bullet in his head.

As I walk down the sidewalk, I hear one of his homeboys ask, "Who's that bitch?"

Cam replies, "My lil' old-school freak."

I grit my teeth and shake my head. *You wish.*

When I get in my car, that uneasy feeling creeps back in, like I'm being watched again. The hair on my arms stands up. I keep my head on a swivel, but there are too many people hanging around to track everyone. Nobody seems focused on me, yet my nerves won't settle.

I unlock the door and slide into the driver's seat. Before I can put the key in the ignition, both the rear and passenger doors fly open.

What the fuck?

A young teen with a blue bandanna covering his face drops into the passenger seat, a pistol aimed straight at me. "Bitch, don't move, or I'll blow your brains out your top!" he snaps.

I place my hands on the steering wheel as his homeboy slides into the back seat. The cold barrel presses against the back of my neck.

"Listen. You don't want to—"

"Bitch, don't say shit. You say one more word, I'ma bust your shit to the white meat."

I shut my mouth and try to think. My gun is wedged at my lower back. *So close, but so far.*

Maybe Cam will come outside. Maybe he'll see what's going on and shut this down. I just have to stay alive a little longer.

"Crank the car up. We going for a little ride," the one in the front says.

Shit.

I do what he says. The engine turns over. "Get on Mesa, and make a right."

"Come on—" I start, but he cuts me off.

"What the fuck I just tell you? You think this shit a game? Don't talk unless I tell you to," Front Seat orders.

My hands start shaking. I should've never come out here like this. But I knew Cam wouldn't have spoken to me if I showed up as a cop.

"Make a left up here," he says.

I obey. After about ten minutes, he tells me to turn onto a dirt road off the Beltway. It leads into tall, thick grass. Gravel crunches beneath the tires as the car rattles forward.

"Stop here."

I hit the brakes and cut the engine.

"Take off your watch and turn your pockets inside out."

I slip off my Marc Jacobs watch and hand it over, then flip my pockets. "That's all I got," I say.

The one in the back opens his door and steps out.

"Get out," Front Seat says.

I open my door and step out. Front Seat slides into the driver's seat and looks at his homeboy.

"Walk her off about twenty feet before you do it. Once you take care of her, we'll scratch off."

My heart starts pounding out of control. I'm seconds away from dying. I need to do something. *Fuck.*

If my gun wasn't tucked into my lower back, I would've already made a move.

"Move," Backseat says, pressing the gun to the back of my head.

I force my legs forward. They feel heavy, like concrete. Then suddenly, a phone rings.

"Hello," Front Seat answers. "Huh? Say what? Hell nah. You for real?"

Something tells me this is my opening. My only chance.

Just as I start to shift, Front Seat yells, "Hold up, cuz! Don't kill her!"

"Huh? Why not?"

"That was Cam on the phone. He said Ze Ze and Draco told him we snatched up some bitch that came out his spot. Cam says she the law."

"What? You serious?"

I close my eyes, relief crashing over me. *Thank you, Jesus.*

"Yeah. Cuz says she's a detective."

"Man, Cuz. We fucked."

***

"Look, fellas, we good. Y'all didn't know," I tell them. "Just give me back my stuff, and we'll act like this never happened."

"Fuck, fuck, fuck," Backseat keeps muttering. They've realized I'm an officer and now understand they bit off more than they could chew.

Backseat looks at Front Seat, fear written all over his face. Now that I really see them, neither one of them looks older than twenty. Front Seat studies me for a moment, thinking. "Look, we'll let you go, but you gotta drop us back off at the crib."

If this weren't so serious, I'd be laughing at how absurd this whole situation is. "Sure. I don't have a problem with that," I tell him.

Front Seat slides back into the passenger seat. Backseat and I get back in the car. With both of their guns still trained on me, I drive us back to the apartments where they grabbed me.

When we pull up, Cam and a few of his homies are already outside, waiting. From the looks on their faces, they're not pleased with what these youngsters pulled. The stares don't go unnoticed. I hear the one in the passenger seat curse under his breath. It's clear they're about to catch hell for this mistake.

As they step out, Cam and I lock eyes. I nod in gratitude before pulling off. He could've easily let whatever those teens had planned play out. I would've been dead, and Cam would've been free of suspicion. Nobody even knew I went over there.

I guess you could say I owe him one. Still, if he turns out to be the one who killed Rachel Willis, I won't hesitate to take him down—even if it hurts.

Chapter 5

I'm still shaken from what happened the other night. I could've easily been killed. The wild part is that the same man who made the call that saved my life might be the one I have to put away.

Rrring. Rrring.

My office phone rings. "Hello?"

"Detective Gordon, can you please come to my office?"

My lieutenant doesn't sound happy.

Mays has been my superior since I came into Homicide. Even though we've bumped heads before, I still respect his leadership.

Knock, knock.

I tap lightly on his door, but it swings open. Standing there is Lt. Anders, a smug look plastered on his face.

"Gordon," he mutters as he brushes past me.

"Come in, Detective," Mays calls.

I step inside carefully. "Is something wrong, Lu?"

"Have a seat."

I do, bracing myself.

"I respect you too much to dance around the issue," he says. "What's going on with this Blackwell case? From where I'm sitting, we've got Gerald Blackwell dead to rights. Motive. Murder weapon. DNA. The only thing missing is an eyewitness. So why am I hearing that you're still pushing this investigation when we've got other pressing matters?"

The pressing matters he's referring to happened two nights ago. A twelve-year-old girl was kidnapped while walking home from school, beaten and strangled, then dumped behind an industrial AC unit.

"I understand, Lu. But I honestly don't believe Blackwell did it." *Well, not that Blackwell anyway.*

"So, you want to waste department resources and deny the family justice, based on a hunch? With no physical evidence to back it up?"

"Well, the examiner said—"

He cuts me off.

"Look, Gordon. You're a damn good detective. Normally, I'd tell you to trust your instincts. But upper brass is pushing hard to wrap this case up. The victim's husband is a twenty-plus-year veteran who made a lot of friends along the way. I don't want to hear anything else about exonerating Blackwell. The evidence points to him, and that's that. The State is taking this to the grand jury tomorrow. Gerald Blackwell will be officially indicted for capital murder."

"But, Lu—"

"No buts, Gordon. This case is closed, and you're dismissed," he says with finality.

I shut my mouth, stand up, and walk out of his office.

I can't shake the feeling that Lt. Anders has something to do with this. I understand the need for closure, but what about the integrity of justice? It feels like they don't care whether the man is innocent or not.

I end up back in my office, sitting at my desk, wondering, *Where do I go from here? Do I leave it alone? Trust the legal system?* If he's innocent, then he should be acquitted.

But then, I think about my baby daddy, Jessy. All he was doing was protecting his woman from an overly aggressive pursuer. Sure, he went too far, but he didn't deserve fifty years. Just thinking about it makes me sick. All of it could've been avoided if I had been more of a woman. I close my eyes and drift back to where everything started to go wrong.

October 2007.

"Unique, why the hell you playing with your food? Don't tell me you tryna be like one of them skinny, White girls in them Playboy magazines," Sanders called from across the table.

She and I were on a double date. She'd been hooking up with one of the guys we completed basic training with—a tall, brown-skinned, curly-haired dude from Memphis. I was with Sergeant Brown. This was our third date. I wasn't eating because I was nervous as hell, not because I thought Brown would hurt me, but because I was really feeling him, and I was scared I'd do something I would regret, like sleeping with him.

Brown turned out to be an attentive listener. He was funny and always made me feel like I was the most important person in the room. What started as a pity date turned into something real. We were on number three, and I was seriously considering giving him some coochie.

Aside from one incident senior year when a guy ate me out, I never cheated on Jessy. I hadn't had sex since I left for basic training. My first leave was only a couple of weeks away.

We were at a soul-food spot off of base called Two Souls, One Heart. As the night wound down, it became clear that I was either going to put up or shut up.

"Excuse me, miss, can we get the check?" Brown asked the light-skinned waitress.

I shot Sanders a look. Before we came out, we talked about the possibility of me sleeping with Brown.

"Girl, go for it. Your dude will never know unless you tell him," she urged. "I'm pretty sure he back home getting his dick wet anyway."

Is he cheating on me? If he is, how can I be mad? He's home, taking care of our daughter, while I'm out on a date, probably about to let another man have his way with me.

The check came. Brown paid, and we all headed to our cars.

When we got to the hotel, my nerves were jumping like jackrabbits.

"You a'ight?" Brown asked, picking up on my energy.

"Yeah. I'm good. I just need a drink."

He grabbed a bottle of Cîroc from the backseat, and we headed inside.

The moment we stepped into the room, I excused myself. I stood in front of the mirror, staring at my reflection.

Girl, get it together. It's just sex, *I told myself.*

When I went back out, Brown was already waiting. Shirtless. Muscles tight. Abs defined. He handed me a cup of vodka and cranberry. I downed it in two gulps, feeling the liquor warm me from the inside out.

Brown took a couple of shots, then walked toward me until we were inches apart. I smelled his breath as he leaned in to kiss me. His tongue slipped into my mouth, and my body lit up. His hands moved to my shoulders, and the straps of my dress slid down, pooling at my feet.

In nothing but a black lace thong, my C-cups hung free. Brown leaned in, grabbed my right breast, and pulled my nipple into his mouth. I moaned, gripping the back of his head.

My juices flowed freely, causing my panties to stick to my coochie. Brown gently pushed me back until I was lying flat on the bed. There was a savage hunger in his eyes. He unbuttoned his slacks, peeled his boxer briefs down, and I finally got an up-close view of what he was working with. Very nice.

He crawled onto the bed and peppered me with kisses. First, my neck and ears, and then he worked his way down until he was face to face with my peach. My breath caught as his lips wrapped around my clit, sucking and slurping. When I felt his long fingers slide inside me and massage my G-spot, I exploded.

"Aaaghh, shit!" I cried out as my orgasm detonated.

Brown spent the next four hours fucking me into oblivion.

The next day, we all went our separate ways. I couldn't help but feel a little shameful, especially when I spotted a picture that Jessy and I took with Shantel right before I left for basic training. Well, what was done was done.

I had to admit, it was fun as hell. At first, I convinced myself it was just a one-time thing. If he called, I'd tell him we couldn't see each other anymore. But the minute Brown called to set up another rendezvous, I almost broke the phone to respond.

Present Day

I wipe the tear that slips free and runs down my face. I don't give a fuck what Lt. Mays or anyone else says. I'm not about to let another innocent Black man get railroaded by the system. If I'm right, and Gerald Blackwell is innocent, I'll do whatever I have to do to make sure he's released.

I pull the diary from my bag and work on the next entry. It takes a little over an hour to decode, but when I finish, it reads:

July 7.

I finally told Gerald that I'm pregnant and the baby is his. Understandably, he's skeptical. I am staying under the same roof as my husband. Besides the time when Cam and his friend assaulted me, I haven't had intercourse with any other man but Gerald. He says he will leave his disgusting ass girlfriend Tierra, but we'll see. I really love Gerald and want to spend the rest of my life with him. I just don't know how to break things off with Ed. Just thinking about what will happen when I do gives me chills.

So, Gerald told Rachel he was going to leave Tierra.

I want to go see him at the jail, but I know there'll be a visitor log I'll have to sign. Someone will definitely be watching it. I don't want to expose myself too soon.

That leaves only one option. Tierra.

I check the time. *10:45 p.m.* I won't make the same mistake twice. I'll go see her tomorrow before work.

I close the journal and get ready to head home. Before I leave, I stop by Carter's office to say goodbye. I accidentally walk in on him having a heated conversation with his wife.

"Liz, I told you before, stop being paranoid. I'm at work, where I always am," he says.

I tap lightly on the door. Carter turns and holds up a finger, signaling me to wait. I give him a minute to collect himself. While I wait, my eyes wander around his office. I notice a picture of him, his wife, and their new baby girl, Carroll.

For a split second, I imagine what our baby would've looked like. I shake the thought away.

Get a grip, Unique, I scold myself. *The man is married, and you're cool with his wife.*

Carter ends the call, exhales, and pinches the bridge of his nose.

"Trouble in paradise?" I ask.

"Yeah. Liz thinks these late nights at the office mean something else. That I'm sleeping around."

I blink, surprised. "What? Are you serious? If you're cheating, you're the most successful cheater I know, because even I didn't have a clue."

"You need to tell her that," he says flatly.

"I don't know how much that would help. She probably already thinks you're cheating with me."

"Actually, she doesn't. Or if she does, she doesn't say it." I hear the hurt in his voice. Being faithful and still accused of cheating has to sting. "Well, enough about me. You headed home?"

"Yeah. I'm going to call it a night."

"Okay. I'll see you tomorrow. Drive safe," he tells me.

"Thank you. I will." Before I make it all the way out of the office, he calls me back.

"Hold on a second. I meant to talk to you about the Blackwell case."

I pivot and face him. "What about it?"

"Well, it's well known you're still working on it. Lt. Mays made a comment about suspending you if you don't drop the case. I've been covering for you as much as I can, but you need to be honest with me. Are you making any progress?"

I hesitate. I trust Carter, but if he's questioned by our superiors, he'll have to tell the truth. He has a family to support. So, I give him enough to earn his cooperation, but not enough to wreck his career.

"I have a new lead I'm following up on tomorrow."

"Okay. So, you going to tell me about this new lead?"

"Of course. I just don't want to jump the gun. Let me check it out first. If it pans out, I'll bring it to you, and we can brainstorm."

He looks a little hurt. He knows I'm holding back, but he also knows why.

"A'ight. Just keep me posted. Don't forget, we have to go see Mandy's seventh-grade teacher tomorrow."

Mandy is the twelve-year-old girl who was beaten and murdered a few nights ago. From everything we've gathered, the killer knew her. Watched her. Waited. Then struck as she walked home from school.

"I got you. While I'm on the clock, I'm all about Mandy. I won't deprive her of that."

"Thank you," he says genuinely.

I head out into the cold night air. The wind cuts through my jacket and sinks into my bones. My hands shake as I pull out my keys and hit the alarm.

That familiar feeling of being watched creeps over me again. Instinctively, I reach into my jacket and brush the grip of my Sig. No matter how hard I try, I can't pinpoint the source of my unease.

You're letting the job get to you.

I clear my head and get into the car. I start the engine, crank the heater, and sit there for a moment, letting the warmth soak into my body.

Bump.

Something hits the back of my car.

I glance in the rearview mirror and see a shadow move across my back windshield. My heart jumps. I grab my pistol, click the safety off, and jump out.

I scan the parking lot. Nothing. No movement. My breath fogs the air as I struggle to steady it. My heart pounds. My palms sweat despite the cold. I'm no stranger to danger, but an unseen threat shakes me to my core.

I close my eyes and force the paranoia down. "Unique, get a handle on this. There's nobody there. It's all in your head," I say aloud.

I get back in the car.

The entire drive home, I check the rearview mirror for any sign of a tail. Nothing. When I finally pull into my driveway, relief floods me. As an officer who puts her life on the line daily, the only thing to hope for is making it home.

Now that I have, I pause to calm myself. The last thing I want is to bring that energy inside. I grab my bag and step through the door, ready to take on my other job.

Mom.

Chapter 6

I move through the house slowly, my footsteps light. It's dead quiet, but I know I'm not alone. I check the time. *2:45 a.m.*

The kids are asleep.

Then I smell it—that sharp, metallic scent. I pray it isn't what I think it is, even though I already know the truth. My grip tightens around my pistol.

Wearing nothing but a sports bra and boy shorts, I inch forward, careful with every step.

Clink.

Something falls in the kitchen.

My heart nearly jumps out of my chest. I pray I don't see what I think I will. *My kids.* That's all I can think about. I pray they're alright.

I round the last corner leading into the kitchen. I still my nerves, tighten my grip on my pistol, and swing it around.

What I see destroys me.

My kids are lying on the kitchen floor, bathed in a pool of blood. My heart drops. I feel lightheaded. Stab wounds cover their chests, stomachs, necks, and arms.

"Oh my God," I croak.

My babies were butchered.

Before I can take a step, someone grabs me from behind. I freeze. A gloved hand clamps over my mouth. I see the other arm lift, a butcher knife clenched tight. Half a second later, the blade comes flying toward my gut and—

"Aaahh, shit!" I scream as I jolt awake.

I check the clock. *3:42 a.m.*

My underwear is soaked with sweat. So are the sheets. I grab the glass of water from my nightstand and down it in one gulp.

I close my eyes, thanking God it was just a dream, then force myself out of bed. Even though I know it wasn't real, I still need to check on my kids.

I change out of my damp clothes, throw on a terry cloth robe, and head to my son's room.

Normally, he keeps his door locked, but tonight it isn't. I twist the knob and peek inside. Ka'Darious is face down, knocked out cold, drooling on his pillow. Relief washes over me. I close the door quietly and head to check on my hardheaded daughter.

Of course, she's not home.

I turn back toward my room, but something tells me to lock the windows. As I'm securing them, I notice a dark-red Cadillac SRX parked in front of my house. I've never seen that car on my street or anywhere in the neighborhood.

I quickly throw on jeans and a sweater, grab my pistol from the dresser, slip on sneakers, and head out the back door. I don't want whoever it is to see me coming and take off before I can identify them.

I move along the side of the house and approach the Cadillac from the rear. As I get closer, I can tell someone is still inside.

When I get within a few feet, what I see makes my stomach turn.

My nineteen-year-old daughter, Shantel, has her face in a man's lap, bobbing up and down. His head is thrown back, his hand under her skirt, touching her. I'm worried sick about her, and she's out here doing this in front of my house.

I consider smashing the window with the butt of my gun, but instead, I grab the door handle. To my surprise, it isn't locked. The interior light snaps on, illuminating the whole car.

"What the fuck?" the man says, slamming back against the driver's door when he sees a gun pointed at his head.

And I'm just as shocked to see he isn't her boyfriend, Mayo.

When Shantel lifts her head and sees me, she instantly gets defensive, like I'm the one invading her privacy.

"Momma, what the hell?"

"What the hell?" I snap. "What you mean, what the hell? Shantel Frazier, if you don't get your ass out this car—" I hate embarrassing my kids, but I'm so angry I could pop her in the mouth for disrespecting my house and herself.

She folds her arms and stares at me defiantly. That's when I snap. I grab her by the weave and yank her out of the car.

She immediately starts fighting, scratching at my arms as I drag her. "Let me the fuck go! Get off me!" she screams.

I know our relationship is going to suffer because of this, but right now, I'm too angry to care. As she struggles, the man steps out of the car, clearly wanting to make sure she's okay. He takes two steps toward us.

I raise my gun. "Don't you fucking come any closer," I growl, itching for a reason to send him to his maker.

Now that he's out of the car, he isn't bad-looking. But seeing him with his cock in my daughter's mouth doesn't allow me to appreciate his good looks. Instead, all I see is red.

He throws his hands up in mock surrender.

"It's all good. I don't want any trouble."

"Look, man. Whoever you are, I suggest you leave and don't come back around my house."

I pull the hammer back to further drive home my point. He wisely jumps in his car and peels off. As soon as Shantel and I make it into the house, I go in.

"Shantel, I can't believe your ass is out there like this. You know I taught you better than that. You in front of my house, sucking some dude's dick in his car. It's like you don't have any respect for yourself."

"Momma, I'm grown. You act like I'm some lil' girl or something. What I do is my business."

"Oh, yeah? Well, as long as you under my roof, you are my business."

"Well, fine. I won't live under your roof then."

Shantel has never been away from home any more than a few days. Honestly, I feel like she's bluffing.

"Okay, well, get your shit and get the hell out of my house," I tell her.

She looks shocked at first. I know she assumed that I would try to convince her to stay. When she sees that I'm serious, she storms out of the living room. I'm left to stew in my decision. I fight back tears. I'm trying as hard as I can. It's tough, being a single black mother, trying to raise two bad-ass kids, while trying to hold down a man who's basically got a life sentence, all while being a homicide detective.

I wipe my face, refusing to let them fall. I head to my room, strip down, and hop in the shower.

I need some comfort.

It's been a while since I've had sex—or just laid in bed with a man. People don't realize that being a strong, independent woman isn't natural. A woman needs a man, and a man needs a woman. That's the natural order of things, and I've gone months without that intimate contact. It's doing something to me biologically.

I step out of the shower, get dressed, and pour myself a glass of Chardonnay. I decide to go ahead and do some more research, pull the diary out, and decode a few more pages.

July 3

Today I went by Gerald's house because he hasn't been answering the phone. Ever since I told him I was pregnant, he's been real standoffish. My plan was to just sit and wait until he came outside, follow him until he parked somewhere, then we would talk. When I pulled up, I noticed his car was gone. I debated waiting, but when I saw his brother drive up,

I decided it was better to just leave. That guy gives me the creeps. It's taking everything in me, not to file charges against him. I don't want to create a rift between Gerald and his brother.

Cam claims she's making the accusations up, but it seems to me that she believes it occurred. One thing is for sure. I need to go see Tierra first thing in the morning.

Beep, beep.

The alarm on the house alerts me that someone just opened the front door. I peek through my bedroom blinds and spot Mayo's candy-red Buick Park Avenue, parked in front of the house.

What the fuck? Shantel's waddling with trash bags full of clothes.

This girl is actually leaving.

I hurry up and throw some jeans and a T-shirt on, rush downstairs, but by the time I make it outside, the car's gone. I pull my phone out and dial my daughter's number.

Straight to voicemail.

She blocked me.

I go back inside, feeling pissed, disrespected, and abandoned. I start to grab my gun and my holster, but remember, *she's grown.* If this is what she wants, so be it. I can't hold her hand her entire life. She'll have to learn one way or another.

I head towards Ka'Darious's room, twist the knob, and push the door open slightly. He's still asleep, still drooling all over his pillow. I can't help but think, *he looks just like his daddy.*

A slight pang pricks my heart. Why does life have to be so hard? I head to my room, finish my Chardonnay, and crawl into bed. The last thing I think before sleep takes me is, *I hope Shantel will be safe.*

I'm up at five thirty and out the door by six. It's early, but I need to stop by Tierra and Gerald's place to ask her a few questions. I don't know if she's aware of the affair, so I'll have to be careful with how I word things.

As I turn into the neighborhood, crack addicts and gang members litter the streets. I park and holster my gun, then grab my detective badge and hang it around my neck before stepping out of the vehicle. *I refuse to make the same mistake twice.*

I approach the front door and immediately catch the unmistakable smell of PCP in the air. *Knock, knock, knock.*

I glance at my watch. "I hope she's here," I mumble to myself.

Knock, knock, knock.

"Who is it?" she groans from behind the door.

"Detective Gordon."

The locks click, and Tierra opens the door, wearing a sports bra and black, lace boyshorts.

"How are you, Ms. Mason? I was hoping to ask you a couple of questions."

"About what?"

"The Rachel Willis incident."

At the mention of Rachel's name, her mouth twists.

She knows.

She studies me for a moment, then steps aside and lets me in. I take note of the place as I walk through. The house looks cleaner than it did when we served the warrant on Gerald.

Something feels off, like something that used to be here isn't anymore. I shake the feeling and take a seat, waiting for her to do the same.

"So, what's up, Detective? What do you need to ask me?"

"First, I want you to know that, even though Gerald is in custody, I'm working to make sure we have the right person responsible. The only way I can do that is if the people I talk to are completely honest with me."

"Okay," she says, almost eager.

"Let's start with what you know about Rachel Willis."

"Not much. I know she was a White woman who worked at the law firm Gerald used for his manslaughter charge. I know she got killed. That's it." Tierra Mason is a terrible liar. Or maybe I'm just very good at reading people. It's obvious she knows more, but she isn't ready to say it. She flips the script. "How much time are they trying to give Gerald?"

"There's no plea on the table. They upgraded the charge to capital murder. It's either life or death."

She doesn't look surprised.

She already knew.

Before she can ask anything else, I press her. "Where were you on the night of December twelfth?"

"I was here, waiting on Gerald to come back from the store."

I catch the undertone in her voice.

Disdain.

She doesn't believe he was at the store either.

"How long was he gone?"

She snorts. "Like an hour and a half."

I jot it down. Gerald must have been with Rachel and told Tierra he was running an errand. I spend the next thirty minutes trying to pull something useful from her. Eventually, I get up to leave, feeling like I've hit a wall. As I walk toward the door, it clicks.

The pictures.

Last time we were here, photos of Gerald and Tierra were everywhere. Now, they're gone.

I don't mention it. I file it away.

"One more question, Ms. Mason. When was the last time you went to visit Gerald?"

"I haven't."

She closes the door.

I sit in my car for a moment before starting it, replaying the interview in my head. Something isn't right. The coldness in Tierra's tone has my instincts screaming. As I pull away, one thought keeps circling.

There's a deeper secret at play.

Chapter 7

As soon as I walk into my office and sit down, Carter pokes his head inside. "We have to go see Mandy's teacher, Vince Thomas," he says, reading from his notepad.

Carter agreed to cover for me on the Amanda Stanley case while I put in extra hours to try to figure out what really happened to Rachel Willis.

I feel a little guilty for not giving Mandy my full attention. Even though it might seem like I value Rachel more, that couldn't be further from the truth.

"Okay, let's go," I say, throwing on my coat. Something clicks in my head. I turn back around, open my bottom drawer, and pull out Rachel's diary. I know the answers to her murder are buried in these pages, and I can't afford to lose it, especially now that I feel like I'm finally making progress.

As we pass the Narcotics division, Lt. Anders looks right at me and says, "Wassup, Carter?" as he walks past us. Carter glances back at me with a look of pity. I shake my head, letting him know I don't care. No matter how good a detective I am, the good-ole-boy establishment will never see me as an equal, not as a Black woman.

So, Anders not speaking to me doesn't bother me. I have a feeling he's the one who pushed my lieutenant to rein me in. I don't know why he's so determined to keep me off this case, but I'll find out.

About twenty minutes later, Carter and I arrive at a modest, one-level brick home in the Woodforest subdivision.

Only one car sits in the driveway: a dark-green Toyota Camry that looks about ten years old, rust creeping along the edges of the door frames.

In the yard, a patch of grass has died, replaced by a small mound of dirt.

Carter and I walk up to the front door.

Knock, knock, knock.

It doesn't take long for Vincent Thomas to answer.

He's a middle-aged White man with a protruding belly, receding hairline, hairy forearms, and a crooked left eye. Carter takes the lead. "How are you doing, Mr. Thomas? I'm Detective Carter. We spoke on the phone, and this is my partner, Detective Gordon. May we come in?"

"Sure. Sure. I apologize for the mess," he says as we follow him inside.

The first thing that hits me is the smell. Without even seeing them, I know he owns at least two or three cats. The place reeks of cat piss and wet fur.

Right on cue, three of them emerge from a back bedroom.

"Would y'all like something to drink?" he offers.

"Oh, no, thank you," we say at the same time.

There's no way I'd accept anything from this man, even off duty. Something about him makes my skin crawl.

Thomas sits down, and Carter begins. "What can you tell us about Amanda Stanley?"

He takes a deep breath as if it pains him to speak. "I don't know a lot. I had her in seventh-grade English. She was naturally smart, but about a month into the semester, she started acting out."

"Acting out how?" I ask.

"She started sleeping in class. When I addressed it, she'd curse at me and get irate. Then she just stopped coming altogether. About two weeks later, they found her dead."

As I jot down notes, Carter continues. "Did you ever contact her parents about her behavior?"

"I contacted her mother once. She said she would handle it. After that, Amanda stopped coming to class. Sometimes, I feel like it's my fault. If I hadn't told her mom, she might still be alive."

"Mr. Thomas, you did the right thing," I tell him. "As a parent and as an officer, I'd want a teacher to do the same if my child was showing that kind of behavior."

He gives me a small nod, gratitude flickering across his face.

We spend the next thirty minutes covering anything that might help: her friends, other teachers, and whether she had a boyfriend, anything that could point us closer to the truth.

Once we collect all the information we can, we head out to see Mandy's mother, Evelyn Stanley. Evelyn is a petite woman with a big attitude and an even bigger addiction. At forty years old, drugs and hard living have aged her at least ten years. Ashy skin and vacant gums tell the story. She's well past her prime but still manages to draw enough interest to fund her habit.

Carter and I pull into the Timber Run Apartments at Woodforest and Grand Oaks, not surprised to see people loitering everywhere, bad-ass kids down to their ratchet-ass parents.

A few years back, a young Blood member burned down part of the complex, killing an elderly woman. Since then, property values have plummeted.

Carter parks, and we step out. As soon as residents spot us, many scatter like roaches, ducking into their apartments and slamming doors behind them.

We approach apartment number 1010.

Knock, knock, knock.

I glance at Carter. "Maybe she's not here," I say.

He shrugs.

We're about to leave when the locks start clicking, and the door slowly cracks open. Evelyn peers out through a narrow gap, eyes wide. The pungent smell of crack smoke pours out of her small, dingy apartment. When she realizes we're police, she tries to slam the door shut, but Carter pushes it back open, causing her to stumble backward.

I lift my hands. "Look, Evelyn. We're not here for that. We don't care about you getting high. We just want to ask you some questions about your daughter, Amanda."

At the mention of her daughter, pain flashes across her face. Mandy was her only child, and no matter how much she gets high to numb it, there's no escaping that kind of loss.

Evelyn studies us, then scans her apartment, clearly checking to make sure nothing incriminating is lying around. Once she's satisfied, she steps aside and lets us in.

Before sitting down, I take in the apartment—beige couches with burn holes dotting the cushions. Evelyn drops onto one and tries to cross her legs, attempting dignity, but her dirty jeans and greasy T-shirt ruin the effort.

I take the lead. "Evelyn, when was the last time you saw your daughter?"

Without hesitation, she answers, "She went to school that morning."

"Did she ride the bus, or did you take her?"

"She rode the bus." Her hands twist together, nerves mixing with whatever she's high on.

"So, you saw her get on the bus?" I ask.

She looks away. This is something she's probably tortured herself over since the day Mandy was found. Her head shakes slowly as tears well up.

I make sure we're clear. "So, you didn't see your daughter get on the bus that morning?"

"No," she whispers.

Carter shakes his head slightly, disgusted. I can almost hear his thoughts. *Because you were high as hell.*

My chest tightens for this woman—losing your only child because addiction stole your awareness. Still, I have to keep going.

"Do you remember getting a call from one of her teachers, Mr. Thomas?"

She turns the name over in her mind, then shakes her head. "No. I never got a call from any teacher."

I'm taken aback. "Are you sure? It was about Mandy's behavior in class."

She shakes her head again. "I'm sure. If someone had called me, I would've said something to her. The only call I got from the school was the day she died."

I exchange a confused look with Carter as he writes it down.

"What about friends or boyfriends?" he asks. "Anyone who might help us?"

"She had a friend named Lisa," Evelyn says. "She stays at Woodforest Chase Apartments, in the front, right by the Metro bus stop."

I jot the information down before Carter and I make our way out the door. As soon as we reach the bottom of the stairs, a dark-blue Taurus creeps past. A chill runs through my bones. I know that car; I just can't place where from.

As it rolls by, I lock eyes with the occupants—two Black males, early to mid-twenties. A blue bandanna hangs from the rearview mirror. They stare Carter and me down, malice written all over their faces. *Could this be the same car that followed me that night?*

I watch the taillights disappear as they exit the complex.

"Gordon? Gordon?"

I snap out of it as Carter calls my name. "Huh?"

"You alright?"

"Yeah, I'm good. What were you saying?"

"We can't just question Lisa if she's a minor. We need to locate her parents and go through them," he says.

"Of course. We don't want some high-priced mouthpiece getting her statement thrown out," I reply.

We get into the sedan and head back toward the precinct. The entire drive, my mind stays stuck on that navy-blue

Taurus and the men inside it. I'm almost certain it's the same car that followed me a few nights ago. *What was it doing over there?*

Since my interview with Tierra, something has been bothering me. I decide to go see Gerald. Something tells me Tierra knows more than she's letting on. It makes me wonder if Gerald told her about Rachel. And if not, how did she find out?

I have no doubt the higher-ups are monitoring Gerald's visitation, waiting to see if I show up again. I make my way to the seventh floor.

"Blackwell. Gerald Blackwell," I tell the deputy at central command.

"Booth number four," she replies.

I take a seat in the attorney's booth and wait for them to bring him out. My thoughts race. *Cam claims Rachel lied about the assault. Ed was out of town, fishing with Lt. Anders. Tierra claims she knows nothing. And all the evidence still points to Gerald Blackwell.*

Shackled hand to foot, Gerald is escorted in. The stress shows in his weight loss, but he's still ruggedly handsome. The deputy shuts the door behind him, and Gerald takes a seat.

"Hey, Gerald."

"Wassup, Detective. I didn't think you were coming back up here."

"Why you say that?"

"One of your coworkers came to see me. Asking about our visits."

I straighten up. "Coworker? Who?"

"I think his name was Anders."

My jaw tightens. "What did he say?"

"He wanted to know why you kept coming to see me. Asked a lot of questions about Rachel."

Now I'm heated. It's common knowledge not to step on another detective's toes. On top of that, Anders works

Narcotics. This is Homicide. There's no legitimate reason for him to be questioning Gerald unless something else is going on.

"What did you tell him?" I ask sharply.

Gerald curls his lip. "What did I tell him? You're the first cop I've ever said more than four words to. Everybody else gets 'I want my lawyer.'"

I can't hide my relief. The last thing I need is Anders or anyone else knowing what I'm working on. Their eagerness to pin this murder on Gerald has me questioning the integrity of the entire case.

"Thank you for that," I say. "Look, Gerald, I'm going to be honest with you, and I need that same honesty in return. There are powerful people in this department who don't want to see you free. Rachel's husband is a decorated veteran with a lot of friends on the force. In their eyes, you're guilty. They won't release you unless I can give them an alternative suspect."

He studies me. "So, what do I need to do?"

"First, I need to ask you about your girlfriend, Tierra."

"What about her?"

"Does she know about the affair between you and Rachel?"

"Of course not. That's why I denied knowing Rachel when y'all first pulled up, remember? Why you ask?"

"I went by to talk to her. Even though she denied knowing anything about Rachel, I got the sense she was lying."

"Well, if she knows, it wasn't from me." Something seems to hit him. "That's probably why she hasn't been up here to see me. I've called and left messages. It's like she went cold on a nigga," he says, almost to himself.

"Who all knew about the affair?"

"My brother. But I know for a fact he wouldn't tell her. They can't stand each other."

"Well, maybe your brother told someone who told Tierra," I suggest.

"That's possible. I'll call Cam and see if he talked to anybody about it."

I hesitate, then press forward. "Speaking of Cam, did Rachel ever tell you about an incident that occurred between her and your brother?"

"An incident? Like what?"

"According to her diary, she claims Cam and a couple of his friends drugged and raped her."

Genuine shock crosses Gerald's face. Hurt too. *He had no idea.*

"That's gotta be some kind of mistake. You must've translated that passage wrong," he says quickly.

"I talked to Cam. He admits something happened, but he claims it was consensual."

He leans back, turning the situation over in his head. I stay quiet, giving him space to process. Finally, he looks up.

"You think my brother killed Rachel and put it on me?"

The question lands heavily. If Gerald believes Cam framed him, he could confront him. If Cam is the killer, that confrontation could send him running. That would ruin any chance of catching him before Gerald goes to trial.

"I don't think he framed you," I say carefully. "But I do want to spend more time looking into how he fits into all this. I need your word that you won't say anything about it. The only way to clear you is to find the person who actually did this. We can't do that if people know the police are closing in."

"I got you," he says, but the hurt is still there. The idea that his brother could've killed the woman carrying his child is tearing him up.

After a few more questions, I let him know it may be a while before I can come back. He says he understands, and I head downstairs.

Hearing Gerald ask if his brother could be the killer pushes Cam straight to the top of my list. Still, something else keeps nagging at me, something I can't quite put my finger on. I start the engine and head home.

When I turn onto my street, I immediately notice an unfamiliar car parked in front of one of my neighbors' houses. It has dark, tinted windows. I can't tell how many people are inside. I try to calm my nerves. It could be someone visiting. *This Willis case has me on edge.*

I pull into my driveway, already sensing the house is empty. I open the garage, pull my Altima in, and shut the engine off. After grabbing my things, I head inside. The silence confirms it.

I check my son's room. *Empty*. His bed is unmade, and clothes are scattered everywhere. I fight the urge to snoop for anything illegal. My respect for his privacy wins. *This time.*

I pass Shantel's room. Even though I know she's gone, I still peek inside. Everything is just as she left it. A part of me hoped she'd come to her senses and be asleep in her bed.

All my calls to her go straight to voicemail.

Maybe I was too hard on her.

I push the thought away, strip down to nothing, pour myself a glass of Hennessy, and run a hot bath. As I sink into the water, my mind drifts to Jessy. My right hand slides down to my box. My middle finger parts my folds while my thumb peels back the hood of my clit.

The heat loosens my muscles as I strum myself until I explode, cumming so hard it steals my breath. My body relaxes completely, and at some point, I must have fallen asleep in the tub.

Bssshh!

Glass shatters, and the house alarm starts screaming. I jolt upright, water sloshing everywhere. I jump out of the tub, dripping wet, grab my robe, and rush for my gun. My heart gallops in my chest. I can't tell if I'm shivering from the cold air hitting my skin or from the fear that my nightmare might be real.

Suddenly, the alarm cuts off.

Panic hits me hard. If the alarm doesn't sound long enough, the company won't call to check on me. I grip my Sig with both hands and creep downstairs. Every step makes my heart pound louder.

My palms sweat as I tighten my grip. At the bottom of the stairs, I slow my breathing.

Thud.

Something heavy hits the floor.

"Fuck," a male voice yelps from the kitchen.

I take three steps forward, then press myself against the wall. Whoever's in the kitchen is moving around clumsily. I count under my breath. *One. Two. Three.*

I step out, pistol raised and ready. I almost pull the trigger until I recognize my knuckleheaded son.

"Oh shit, Momma, don't shoot!" he yells.

Relief floods me. I lower the gun, staring at him with equal parts love and fury. "Where the hell have you been?" I ask.

"I was chilling at Steven's house. You said you didn't want him over here, so I went over there."

All I can do is close my eyes and shake my head. I force myself to calm down. "You know what, Ka'Darious? I can't deal with this right now. Clean this mess up and take your ass to bed." I turn and head back upstairs. Once I'm in my room, I drain the tub, clean it, and get ready for bed.

Sleep doesn't come. I pour myself another two fingers of Hennessy and knock it back. As the liquor settles in, I lie there, replaying how close I came to killing my own son. A tremor runs through me. Eventually, my eyelids grow heavy, and I finally drift off.

Chapter 8

It's early morning when Carter and I pull into Woodforest Chase Apartments. Mandy's friend Lisa lives right up front, near the entrance.

Carter parks, and we step out into the cool, crisp eighty-two-degree air. The sun is already up and bright. Carter called ahead and spoke to Lisa's mother. By law, a parent or guardian has to be present when questioning a minor, so we scheduled the interview before Lisa heads to school.

Knock, knock, knock.

"Who is it?" a woman calls out.

"Detective Carter, ma'am."

The locks click, and the door opens. The scent of cinnamon and brown sugar hits my nose.

"Come in," she says. Lisa's mother, Belinda, is a curvy woman with light-brown skin and eyes to match. Her lips are full and pink, and there's a quiet intensity in her gaze. She's a beautiful woman.

As we step inside, I take in the apartment. It feels warm and lived in. Photos of her daughters, Lisa and Taylor, cover the walls, the entertainment center, and the tables.

This woman loves her kids.

"Please, have a seat," she says, disappearing briefly down the hall.

Moments later, she returns with Lisa beside her. The girl looks nervous, and I can't blame her. With everything going on lately, people are more hesitant than ever to trust the police.

"How are you doing, Lisa?" I ask gently. "I'm Detective Gordon, and this is my partner, Detective Carter. We'd like to ask you a few questions about your friend Mandy. Is that okay with you?"

She glances up at her mother for approval. With a subtle nod, Belinda gives her permission to speak freely.

"Yes, it's okay," Lisa answers.

"Were you and Mandy close?" I begin.

"Yes, ma'am. She was my best friend."

"Did she ever tell you anything was wrong? Anything or anybody she might've been scared of?"

Lisa shakes her head but still answers. "No, ma'am."

"When was the last time you spoke to Mandy?"

"The night before she died. She told me she wasn't going to school."

"Did she say why?"

Lisa looks to her mother again. Belinda nods. "She said she was going to meet with a boy."

I feel Carter stiffen beside me.

"Did she tell you the boy's name?"

"No, ma'am. I asked, but she said it was a secret. She said she promised him she wouldn't tell anybody." *Interesting.*

"Did Mandy have any other friends she might have told?"

Lisa thinks for a moment. "We were best friends. If she wouldn't tell me, I don't think she would tell anyone else."

I feel a bit deflated until she adds, "But…"

I perk up. "But what?"

"She had this other dude she used to mess with. He's older than us."

"Do you know his name?" Carter finally jumps in.

"Jacob. He stays in The Oaks of Woodforest." She glances up at her mother again, like she's worried she's said too much. "He's in a gang. He's a Blood."

For some reason, Ka'Darious flashes through my mind. *I wonder if he knows this Jacob.*

Before we get up to leave, something occurs to me. "Lisa, you said he's older. How much older?"

She looks to her mother once more. Belinda nudges her gently. "He's sixteen."

Damn. That means we'll have to locate his parents and go through them.

"Well, thank you so much, Lisa," I say. "You were a big help. Because of you, we're going to find whoever did this to your friend and make sure they go to jail."

She smiles. She loved Mandy and wants justice for her.

I turn to Belinda. "Thank you for allowing us to speak with her."

"No problem. What happened to that little girl isn't right. That could've been Lisa. Mandy was here almost every day. They were like sisters."

"We'll get them," I promise.

Belinda walks us out.

As we get into the car, I notice Lisa watching us from the window. My chest tightens. Losing your best friend like that leaves a scar that never really fades. Thoughts of my daddy creep into my mind, but I shove them away. *This is not the time, Unique.*

Carter turns toward me. "You want to ride over to The Oaks and see if we get lucky?"

"We can do that."

Talking to Lisa has me itching to find the bastard responsible. The longer we wait for procedures, the colder the trail gets. In this job, there's a thin line between reckless and resourceful. A great detective knows how to dance on that line without falling.

We head toward Uvalde.

We turn into the entrance behind where Church's Chicken used to be. About a dozen people are standing around. Some are dressed neutral, but most are draped in red. I remember growing up in the late nineties and early two thousand, when this area belonged to the Crips. Now it's a Blood stronghold.

This also happens to be the same complex Steven is from.

Carter and I sit in the car and observe. Sometimes, if you just sit back and watch, people will give themselves up. Suddenly, an idea hits me. I pull out my phone and call my son.

"Hello," he answers.

"Where you at?"

"Getting ready for school."

"I need a favor. What apartment does Steven stay in?" The line goes quiet. I check the screen to make sure the call didn't drop. "Ka'Darious, you there?"

"Yeah, Momma. Why you want Steven's apartment number?"

"Son, trust me. He's not in trouble. I just need his help finding somebody."

I try to ease his concern.

"Momma, I don't think he'll help. You know how dudes are when it comes to talking to police." *Yes, I do.*

"I understand that. This is about that little girl Mandy."

I remember when Ka'Darious saw the story on the news and asked if I would be getting the case. I told him I didn't know, but probably. His response stuck with me.

"I hope so. So you can slam that sick motherfucker."

I don't approve of his cussing, but I understand his anger. It takes a special kind of twisted person to hurt a child like that. Hearing me say it's about Mandy hits a soft spot.

"He stays in apartment 713."

"Thank you, Son."

"No problem."

Before we hang up, I add, "Make sure you take your butt to school. I don't want any calls saying you didn't show up."

He huffs. "A'ight, Momma. I will."

We disconnect, and I turn to Carter. "Go around to the side of the complex. Apartment 713."

Carter pulls out and heads around the building. When we spot it, he parks but keeps the engine running.

"Let me go in first," I say. "Once I make contact, I'll call you and let you know when to come in. We don't want people spreading word that cops came asking about Steven. That would kill any future interviews."

Carter nods. He gets it.

I remove my badge, take my hair out of the ponytail, slip off my blazer, and undo the top two buttons of my shirt before stepping out.

The Oaks used to be a dangerous complex, the kind you didn't want to be caught in after dark. These days, it's calmer, but caution still matters. I tone down my authority and walk as if I belong here. I'm from the hood, but it's been a long time, and I'm not sure I still look the part.

I reach the apartment without trouble and knock.

Knock, knock, knock.

Rap music blares from inside. I glance at my watch. *6:45 a.m.* Way too early for all that.

I knock again.

The door swings open, and Steven stands there in red basketball shorts, shirtless. I flick my eyes down for half a second, then force myself to look away. *Girl, get it together. He's young enough to be your son.*

"Ms. Gordon, what's good?" he asks. "Something wrong with Kango?"

"No. Ka'Darious is fine. This is about one of your homeboys who stays over here."

He looks surprised. After checking behind me to see who's around, he lowers his voice. "Look, Ms. G, I ain't into ratting. I'm not—"

"I understand, Steven," I cut in calmly. "I'm not asking you to get anyone in trouble. I just need to locate someone so I can ask a few questions. He's not a suspect."

He studies me, not like someone looking at a cop, but like a man looking at a woman. I can tell I've crossed his mind before. I lean into it.

"Steven, I really need your help. If you come through for me, let's just say I'll owe you one."

He reads into it his own way and licks his lips. "Who you looking for?"

"Do you know a kid named Jacob?"

"Yeah. J Boy. He stays by the pool."

"I need to talk to him. Which apartment?"

He grabs himself and smirks. "So, I'll be able to start coming back over to your house?"

I almost laugh at his nerve. For eighteen, he's got plenty of confidence.

"Steven, I don't have a problem with you coming over," I say evenly. "I just don't want my son in trouble, and I don't want drugs or smoking in my house. Other than that, you're welcome." I let a little softness slip into my tone.

He grins. "A'ight. J Boy stays in apartment 1212. If you want, I can call him and tell him to meet you."

"Naw, he's only sixteen. I'll need to talk to his parents. Do you know if they'll be home?"

"I'm pretty sure his dad will be there. He's on disability. His mom died a few years ago, though."

"Well, thank you for that," I say as I head for the door. Before leaving, I glance once more at his print, which seems to have grown during our conversation. *You need to get a grip on yourself, Uniquha.*

When I get back to the car, Carter looks confused. "I thought you were going to call me so I could come in."

"He said he wouldn't talk if anyone else was there," I lie. "Plus, it didn't take long. He said Jacob lives a couple sections over. Apartment 1212. His dad's on disability, so he should be home."

We drive over and park directly in front of Jacob's apartment on the first floor. I check the time. "You think he's already gone to school?"

"I don't know," Carter says. "As bad as it sounds, I hope not."

We get out and approach the door.

Knock, knock, knock.

No answer.

We try again.

Knock, knock, knock.

Still nothing. "Forget it," Carter says. "We'll come back later."

As we turn to leave, a dark-skinned kid about five-ten walks toward us. "If you're looking for my dad, he won't answer. He's in a wheelchair and probably on his meds."

Jacob has a small, nappy fro and acne scattered across his cheeks and forehead. He's holding a grocery bag from the store at the front of the complex.

"Actually," I say, "we're looking for you."

He freezes. "For me? Why?"

"First, we need your dad's permission to talk to you. You think he'll give it?"

He thinks it over, then realization hits. "So what? Y'all cops or something?"

"Yeah, but we're not here to arrest anybody. We just want to ask you some questions about Amanda."

A flicker of sadness crosses his face at the mention of his girlfriend.

"Pops ain't gonna trip," he says. "I pretty much raised myself anyway. Come on."

He unlocks the door and lets us inside a small but cozy two-bedroom apartment. Surprisingly, it's neat and well-kept.

"Aye, Pops, there some cops here to talk to you," Jacob calls out as he disappears down the hall.

Carter and I wait. I glance around and notice framed photos of Jacob's mother throughout the apartment. *She was definitely beautiful.* Losing one parent to death and another to disability is heavy, especially when you're still a kid trying to raise yourself.

Moments later, Jacob's father rolls out in a wheelchair. He's dark-skinned, slightly overweight, with thinning hair and a salt-and-pepper beard. His eyes have a distant, dreamlike quality. What Jacob said earlier echoes in my head. *Probably on his meds.*

I pull out my recorder to document consent.

"How are you doing, Mr…" I start.

"Lackey," Jacob supplies.

"How are you doing, Mr. Lackey?" Carter asks. "We'd like to speak with your son about an ongoing investigation, if that's alright."

Jacob's dad shoots Carter a hard look, then turns to me. "Is he in trouble? He need a lawyer?"

He doesn't trust the White man, I note.

"No, sir," I reassure him. "We just need to ask him about his relationship with Amanda."

He nods slowly. "Alright. You can talk to him."

"Thank you, sir," I say, turning back to Jacob.

"So, Jacob, you and Mandy were boyfriend and girlfriend?"

"Yeah. About six months."

"Where did y'all meet?"

"At the movies. I was there to see *Wakanda Forever*. She was there with her friend Lisa."

After a few basic questions, I lean forward and get to the heart of it.

"Do you remember anything strange going on with Amanda right before she was killed?"

Jacob pauses, thinking it over, then nods. "Yeah. One day, we were chilling, and she kept texting someone back and forth. When I asked who it was, she said it was her aunt. But she'd already told me she didn't really know any of her extended family. When she put her phone down, I checked it."

"And what did the messages say?" I ask.

"I don't know. She deleted them as she read them."

I glance over at Carter. We're thinking the same thing. *Let's just hope whoever it was didn't use a ghost text app.*

"When was the last time you saw her?"

"Two days before she died. We went to Carl's B.B.Q., ate, then came back over here. She walked home around seven."

Jacob's father nods in confirmation. *He must've been here and remembered Mandy staying over.*

I wrap up my questioning, and Carter and I head back to the car. He's already on the phone, working to secure a warrant for her phone records. More than likely, the phone account is in her mother's name or another adult's. Once we identify the account holder, getting the warrant should be straightforward.

As we drive off, my thoughts drift to Shantel. It could have easily been her lying dead behind some A/C unit. I pull out my phone and call her. Straight to voicemail. *Still blocked.*

I exhale, close my eyes, and whisper a quick prayer that she's safe.

Chapter 9

It's been almost a month since Rachel's body was discovered, and I'm forced to work the case in secret. My lieutenant questioned me hard about my visit to the county jail to see Gerald. I told him it was about possible gang connections and other members tied to the murder. I don't think he fully bought it, but he appreciated that I gave him a plausible explanation.

I've stopped reading the diary at work altogether and even bought a replica to leave in the evidence locker. Since I'm the lead detective, no one else should have a reason to dig through it.

Carter and I are still waiting on the warrant for Mandy's phone records. The judge said it should be signed tomorrow, so in the meantime, I've been going through my father's old files.

Since I was a kid, I've been obsessed with solving his murder. That's the whole reason I became a detective. I made a vow that I wouldn't retire until I figured out who killed him. The case is almost thirty years old and colder than Antarctica, but I still haven't given up.

My personal phone vibrates inside my bag. I pull it out and see a private number. Normally, I wouldn't answer, but sometimes, informants call from blocked numbers. I pick up. "Hello?"

No response. Just heavy breathing on the other end. My first instinct is to hang up, but something tells me to listen. I strain for clues, trying to figure out who's playing on my phone. Soft murmurs and low groans follow. If I didn't know any better, I'd think someone was having sex.

Against my will, heat pools low in my body.

I hang up immediately. *What the fuck?*

Right then and there, I realize I need to get laid.

I sit at my desk, thinking it through, deciding exactly who I want. The only question is whether I can pull it off without his wife finding out.

I know it's wrong to sleep with a married man, but what am I supposed to do when those are the only ones showing me real interest? I could easily grab some random guy, but that's never been my style.

I park the car and sit for a few minutes, second guessing myself. *What if he turns me down? What if he can't get away from his wife?*

I kill the engine and check the time before stepping out. *Almost 11:00 p.m.*

I walk up to his door and knock lightly.

Knock, knock, knock.

The temperature has dropped, and I shiver as I pull my jacket tighter around me. Just as I'm about to turn away, the door opens, and a wave of warm air hits my face.

My neighbor, Art, stands there with no shirt and a pair of blue-and-white Polo pajama bottoms.

"Unique, is everything alright?"

Here goes nothing.

"Uhh, … is Daisy home?" I ask.

"Yeah, but she's asleep. She's feeling a little under the weather. Is there anything I can help you with?"

Perfect.

"I'm a very busy woman who doesn't have time to bullshit. Between my kids and my career, I don't have much time to date. I was wondering if we could spend a couple hours in each other's company."

Art looks shocked at first, but then interest starts to gleam in his eyes. Finally, he asks, "When? Right now?"

I look him straight in the eyes. “Yeah. Right now.”

He turns slightly, as if his wife might suddenly appear. After realizing the coast is clear, he turns back to me and thinks it over. “Meet me at the Scottish Inn on I-10 and Normandy.”

Just like that, I’m on my way to have sex with another woman’s husband.

I pull up to the motel and, for a split second, consider standing him up. But then my kitty starts to purr. I haven’t had sex in months. Art is probably going to have a little trouble getting it in.

After purchasing the room, I text him the number. I scrub and clean every nook and cranny, then walk back into the room, still soaking wet.

“Oh shit!” I yelp when I see Art already inside, wearing nothing but a pair of Burberry boxers.

“We gotta hurry,” he says. “Daisy was asleep, but I left her a note saying I ran to the store and to call me if she wakes up and needs something.”

I’m more than okay with that.

Without a word, I stalk toward him, dropping to my knees and tugging at his waistband. Every woman wants a man with enough size to make her cry out, but I still cringe slightly when I see what Art is packing. Semi-erect, he’s about six inches, thick and heavy-looking.

I grip him at the base and take the head into my mouth. An ecstatic moan escapes his lips as I wrap mine around his shaft, stroking him back and forth. Saliva coats his rod, slick and shiny.

Art leans his head back, weaving his fingers through my hair and gripping the back of my skull. He starts popping his hips, pushing deeper, fucking the back of my throat.

Ghlup. Ghlup. Ghlup.

Just the feel of warm meat on my tongue has me dripping something fierce. Once Art is hard as steel, he pulls back, his dick slipping free. I whimper at the sudden loss but perk up when he motions for me to lie back on the bed.

I comply, spreading my thighs and peeling my pussy lips apart.

Art crawls onto the bed and dives headfirst into my box. I feel his sharp intake of breath as he inhales my scent. After inspection, he peels my hood back, exposing my jellybean clit. His tongue flicks across the tip, and my body shivers.

Now it's my turn to grip his head and grind into his hungry mouth.

"Oh my… Oh my." I pant.

Wet slurping sounds fill the room as my orgasm builds. I clutch his head tighter while Art sucks faster, harder.

"Ohhh, shit, I'm cumming. I'm cumming. Don't stop. Fuuucckk!" I cry as my release splashes against his lips and chin.

He laps up every drop before climbing up my body. He sheathes himself as he goes, positioning at the mouth of my coochie.

The moment of truth.

I grab his biceps and brace myself.

"Uggghhh, shit," I hiss as he pushes through, my walls clamping down while he starts pumping back and forth. For the next thirty minutes, he fucks me so good I cum back-to-back.

Suddenly, his phone rings. He recognizes the ringtone and jumps out of my coochie.

"Hello… Hey baby," he says.

I crawl out of bed, peel the wet, soggy condom off, and blow him while he talks to his wife.

Once he gets off the phone, I go into overdrive until he tenses, jerks, then floods my mouth with delicious nectar. With no hesitation, I gulp him down, suckling until he deflates. Only then do I relinquish my hold. Short-winded and fully sated, Art kisses me on the top of my head before washing up and rushing out the door.

I lay in bed, feeling the need to climax once more.

That's what I do.

Afterwards, I get in the shower, clean myself up, and then head home.

The next morning, I wake to find Ka'Darious has already left for school. When I knock on his door, it opens slightly. Now, I've always respected my kid's privacy, somewhat, but something tells me I should do a little snooping. I step into his room. My detective's nose detects a distinct marijuana aroma, not the type of weed that's been smoked, but the type that's fresh.

I've told Ka'Darious repeatedly not to have any drugs in the house.

If he's going to smoke it, do it outside in the backyard, but make sure he smokes it all. I can't afford to have any drugs found in the house. Period.

I search through the dresser, the closet, and under the bed. When I lift the mattress, I get more than I bargained for. Lying there is what looks like half an ounce of weed and a handgun. By the looks of it, it's a Glock .9.

How could he disrespect me like this?

Why the hell does Ka'Darious feel as though he needs a gun? I wonder if he has gotten himself into some trouble. I snatch the gun and weed up and stash them in the tool shed in the backyard. I'm so pissed; it takes me longer than usual to get ready for work. When I do get there, Carter is waiting for me.

"We got the warrant. The phone company's faxing over the entire record for three months' worth of correspondence."

"Good, grab them and meet me in my office," I tell him over my shoulder.

He takes off, and I head to my desk with my bag in tow. Immediately, I notice my desk has been tampered with. When it comes to my belongings, I'm borderline OCD. My papers have been moved, and my drawers have been rummaged through. I have a feeling I know what they were looking for. If I'm right, that means someone has realized the other is a fake. Subconsciously, I pat my bag where the real diary is hidden within a false pocket. I don't have time to contemplate what this means before Carter steps in with the transcripts.

We split them in half. Even though it only covers ninety days, it's still a lot of work. He heads back into his office to comb through his portion, and I sift through mine. Painstakingly, I work my way through text message after text message, conversation after conversation.

Finally, something pops out at me. About a month before she died, Mandy started getting text messages from a new number.

346-....: *Have u ever done anal?*

Mandy: *Hell no. Scarred.*

346-.....: *Don't be. It's really fun.*

My stomach turns at the thought of whoever this is taking little Mandy fast. I start taking notes, documenting each day they were in contact with each other. As I continue to read, the conversations grow more explicit as the days go by.

Then, I see what I'm looking for.

346.....: *R we still on 4 2morrow?*

Mandy: *Yeah. Same spot?*

346.....: *No. Different spot. Remember where we met in the rain?*

Mandy: *Yup. Will b there.*

That was the day before she was killed. According to these records, whoever's on the other side of this 346 number is more than likely responsible for her death. I'm willing to bet this number is a ghost app. Nowadays, it's damn near impossible to track users down.

After I run through my portion of the transcripts, I head over to Carter's office. We both came to the same conclusion. Once Mandy died, her phone received no more calls or texts from that number, like they knew calling her was no use.

She'd been missing for almost a week. Naturally, all her family and friends had been calling and texting, trying to locate her.

We called our team of technicians and gave them the number. Within minutes, they confirmed my suspicions. *An app number.*

Even though it's a deterrent, it's not a dead end. It just means we need to work harder at identifying the caller. Something clicks in my head. I go back to where the caller wrote, *It was nice seeing you today.*

Mandy should have been in school at that time. Something is telling me this is a huge clue as to the identity of the killer. I tell Carter about my hunch, and he agrees it's definitely worth looking into.

Instead of going through the red tape, trying to get the information from the school ourselves, we locate Mandy's mom again and ask her to call the school to inquire about her daughter's attendance record. What we learn leaves me stunned.

Chapter 10

After learning that Mandy was in school all day, and her mom vouched for the fact that she came straight home afterward, that meant the killer must have seen her at school. I highly doubt it was a middle school student, but you never know. That leaves the faculty.

Carter and I agree that, first thing in the morning, we'll head back to Cunningham Middle School to question some of Mandy's former teachers. Right now, I'm ready to call it a night.

I pull into the driveway, feeling emotionally and mentally drained. I glance toward my neighbor Art and Daisy's house. Flashbacks from the night before creep into my head. I know it can't happen again. That was just a desperate attempt to relieve pressure before I exploded.

I park in the driveway instead of the garage and walk into the house, expecting to find Ka'Darious, but he isn't here. I check the time. *11:45 p.m.* He's way past his curfew. I call his phone and get voicemail. I sigh heavily, trying to lower my blood pressure. *This boy is always trying me.*

I head upstairs to wash the day away. When I come back downstairs, Ka'Darious is finally walking his black ass into the house. He's draped in red, a matching bandanna hanging out of his right back pocket. *I know this negro didn't.*

When I get closer, it's even worse. His face is swollen, one eye blackened, and blood smeared across his shirt.

"Ka'Darious, what the hell happened to you?" I nearly scream, panic rising in my chest.

"Nothing, Momma. I'm good. I just wanna shower and go to sleep."

As he talks, I catch the heavy scent of weed and alcohol. He's swaying slightly, struggling to keep his balance.

"No. I need to know what the hell is going on. You come home beat up, and what is this?"

I reach for the bandanna. This little motherfucker actually tries to smack my hand away. I damn near punch him in his mouth. "Nigga, have you lost your motherfucking mind? Don't you ever put your hands on me!" I seethe. I know it was reflex, but I still won't tolerate it.

"I wasn't tryna hit you!" he snaps defensively.

I don't give him time to breathe. "And what were you doing with guns and drugs in my house?"

His eyes widen. "You went snooping through my stuff?" He sounds offended, like his privacy outranks my livelihood.

"Listen, Ka'Darious. My name is on that lease. I'm a detective, an officer of the law. I told you before, don't bring illegal shit into my house. It's like you're doing this on purpose, just to disrespect me."

He sighs and turns his head like he's about to walk away.

"Boy, look at me when I'm talking to you."

"For what? You talking about respect, but you don't respect my space. You leave early in the morning and don't come back 'til damn near midnight. You never here, Momma. But now you wanna pull up like you care about a nig—"

Smack.

The sound echoes through the house. I slap the taste out of his mouth and regret it instantly.

Ka'Darious balls his fists. His mouth twists into something dark and ugly. His body trembles with rage. In that moment, I realize something that chills me to the bone. He's much bigger than me now.

"Unique, don't put your hands on me. I ain't done shit to you. You wanna hit me because I'm telling you the truth," he growls.

For the first time, I fully realize how much damage my son could cause if we actually got into it. He still has at least one more growth spurt coming, but he's already knocking on six feet.

I lock eyes with him, refusing to back down. He needs to understand who's in charge. Finally, he relents and heads to his room, slamming the door behind him. Only then do I allow myself to breathe. My hands won't stop trembling. I immediately pour myself a stiff shot of cognac. *I will definitely need to take him to see his father this weekend.*

After showering, I crawl into bed with a heavy heart. My daughter is gone, and now my son is in a gang. *Why, Lord, must you punish me so?* I close my eyes and drift into a troubled sleep.

The next morning, I wake up drenched in sweat. The same nightmare again. I walk into a bloodbath with both my kids lying out and butchered. I pop an Advil, drink a glass of water, and check the time. *3:50 a.m.* Way too early. There's no way I'm falling back asleep.

I grab my bag, retrieve the diary, and head to work.

August 9

I guess Gerald finally told his ghetto girlfriend. She and a few of her dusty friends cornered me today. I don't know how they found out where I work, but three minutes after I left my job, they jumped out on me at the red light, beating on my windows. Gerald tells me I need a gun. If I would've had one, at least one of those bitches would've been dead. Yeah, I definitely don't need a gun.

So, Tierra did know Rachel.

Even though I already suspected it, seeing it in black and white still shocks me. I close my eyes and replay the interview with Tierra, trying to catch anything I might have missed.

Thump.

A loud noise echoes through the silence.

My eyes fly open. Someone is moving around in the house. I check the time again. *4:20 a.m.* It's way too early for it to be Ka'Darious. I'm always the one waking him up for school.

I sit completely still, praying it's just my imagination.

Thump.

There it is again.

I hop out of bed, grabbing my gun from the nightstand. Déjà vu washes over me as I slowly make my way downstairs, taking steady steps, gripping the weapon with both hands.

I check every room. Nothing.

Finally, I reach my son's door and press my ear against it. He's snoring like a cub. I shake my head at my paranoia and head back to my room to get ready for work. Lately, that's the only place I can find any peace.

I debate leaving the diary at home, but I decide against it. After slipping it into my bag, I head downstairs to wake Ka'Darious for school.

Of course, he doesn't like being woken up almost an hour earlier than usual. Oh well. I need to make sure he's fully awake before I leave. He's still sore about last night.

Something between us has shifted. He's colder now, distant, like he grew into someone else overnight.

"Do you need some money?" I ask once I see he's fully awake.

"I don't need nothing from you, Unique."

I grit my teeth. I want to correct him for calling me by my government name, but I stop myself. There's no law saying he has to call me Momma.

Instead, I exhale and head out the door.

As I step outside, I see Daisy walking toward her car on her way to work. She spots me and lights up.

"Hey, girl, good morning!" she calls out.

I'd rather not speak to her, knowing I had her husband's dick in my mouth less than forty-eight hours ago. Still, I force myself to be cordial.

"Hey, Daisy, you headed to work?" I ask, even though I already know the answer.

"Yeah. I've got six more months before I retire," she says as she opens her car door.

"I know you're happy about that," I tell her as I open my door. We exchange goodbyes, and I crank the engine, letting the heater defrost the windows. As I sit back, I notice the same car from a couple of nights ago parked at the end of the street, sitting idle. It doesn't look like it's moved at all.

I pull out of my driveway and slowly approach the car, easing up so I can get a closer look inside. The tint is too dark, and there isn't enough light, but it appears empty. *They're probably here visiting someone.* I push the thought aside and head to work.

Carter and I pull up to Cunningham Middle School. We need to talk to Mandy's teachers again. Everyone is accounted for except her Social Studies teacher, Mr. Miller.

We ask each of them if they noticed Mandy talking to anyone who might have been too old for her. Every teacher denies seeing anything suspicious. When I question Mr. Thomas about calling Mandy's mother, he remains steadfast in his claim that he did. He even recounts the conversation, word-for-word.

Carter and I finish our interviews, feeling no closer to identifying Mandy's killer.

"It's something we're missing," I say aloud as we sit in the sedan, parked in the school lot.

"I guess we'll have to go back to the precinct and comb through the transcripts again. Maybe something will pop out," he replies.

My mind drifts back to the Rachel Willis case. I need to talk to Tierra, but I'm not sure I should bring my partner. It's not that I don't trust him. I just don't want to jeopardize the case or his career if our superiors decide to make an example of someone.

"Yeah, we should head back," I say.

Once we return, I go straight to my office, grab something, and head right back out. I pass Carter's office on the way.

"Hey, I need to make a quick run. I'll be back in about forty-five minutes," I tell him.

He knows I'm still working the case, but he's smart enough not to ask questions. *Can't tell what you don't know.*

"I'll hold the fort down," he says with that infectious smile of his. For a split second, an image of his soft lips flashes through my mind, but I quickly push it away. I don't know if I'm attracted to Carter as a man or as someone who has my back. Either way, it's been a long time since I've felt that kind of support.

I head downstairs and nearly bump into Lt. Anders as he storms inside. He looks irritated. He doesn't say a word, just grunts and brushes past me.

I'm really starting to dislike that man.

I get in my car and head toward Barrett Station to see Tierra.

As I turn down her street, I notice people everywhere. Dope fiends and dealers line both sides of the road. I pull up to her address and park.

It's midday, so I expect her to be home. As I approach the door, I hear a scream from inside. Instinctively, I draw my firearm. I twist the knob and push the door open, stepping inside. I hear faint voices coming from the back of the house. I can't tell how many people are there, but it sounds like at least one woman. I clear the front of the house, then make my way toward the back.

As I round the corner, laughter fills the air. The bedroom door is slightly open. I catch a glimpse of Tierra talking on the phone, wearing a light-blue dress while rubbing lotion on her arms and legs. Her hair is damp, like she just stepped out of the shower.

I pause, listening.

"Boy, stop playing. You know damn well we don't keep rodents in this house. As many times as you've been over here. Yeah, whatever. Your ass probably left it before you left. Uh huh. Say what? Of course, I had fun. I always have fun when we do our thing."

Whoever she's talking to must have just left, and it sounds like they were intimate.

I quietly back away before she realizes I'm there. Once I make it back outside, I close the door and knock forcefully.

Knock, knock, knock.

Moments later, Tierra answers with her phone pressed to her ear.

"Babe, let me call you back."

She hangs up, and I greet her with a slight smile. "How are you doing, Ms. Mason? We've come across a new development in the case, and I'd like to ask you a few questions."

She stiffens but figures there's no way I could know she approached Rachel Willis near her job. She decides to roll the dice and lets me in.

"Would you like something to drink?" she offers.

"No, thank you," I decline before taking a seat. She sits across from me.

"What's this about?"

"Well, we've learned that you haven't been completely honest with us. Matter of fact, you straight up lied."

Tierra's posture straightens. *Good. I have her attention.*

"Wh-what are you talking about? I haven't lied about nothing?" It comes out more like a question than a statement.

"For one, you did know who Rachel Willis was, including where she worked. In fact, we have footage from a street camera showing you and your friends confronting her." I gamble with the lie. I don't want to expose the diary. That's Rachel's account, and Tierra could easily dismiss it the same way Cam did. But footage sounds concrete enough to make her think twice.

I watch her weigh her options. Her phone rings. She looks at me, silently asking permission to answer. I shake my head slightly. She texts instead. As soon as she finishes, I press on.

"Look, Ms. Mason, you're already in hot water for lying. Now we have footage of you and your friends going after her. How do you think that looks, especially now that she's been murdered?"

Tierra shakes her head. "I didn't kill the bitch."

"Then why did you lie about knowing her?"

"Because."

"Because what?"

"Because she was fucking Gerald, okay? I found out where she worked, but I didn't plan on bringing my girls. They just happened to be in the car when I got the information. So I went to her job, waited until she got off, followed her a couple blocks, then hopped out to talk to her."

Most of this lines up with what I already knew, but what she says next catches me off guard.

"When I pulled up next to her, she rolled her window down and started talking. I asked her straight up if she was fucking Gerald. The bitch laughed in my face and said, 'Of course, I'm fucking him, and he's having my baby.' I thought she was lying until she showed me her stomach. Then she had the nerve to say, 'Don't be mad because a White woman took your man.' That's when I lost it. I tried to snatch her out the car, but she sped off, and we lost her in traffic."

This is the second time someone has contradicted Rachel's version of events, and this time, Tierra did it without knowing what Rachel had written.

I honestly don't know if I believe her. She lied at first, but I can understand why. Still, I can't let up. "If that's all that happened, you should've been upfront from the start. Let me ask you something. How did you find out about Rachel and Gerald? Did he tell you?"

"No, he didn't. I found out from someone else."

"Who?" I push.

"A friend. Look. It doesn't matter who told me. The point is, my supposed man didn't tell me he was fucking that pink bitch and got her pregnant."

As a woman, I know she's hurting. I also know pain like that can push someone too far.

"I'll need the names of the friends who were with you," I tell her. "And don't plan on going anywhere anytime soon."

Her shoulders sag, and I watch the weight settle on her. She knows what that means.

Person of interest.

Whether that turns into suspect is still up in the air.

Her phone vibrates again. I watch as she texts a response. Whoever is calling is persistent. She feels my eyes on her, looks up from the screen, and asks, "Are we done here?"

"Yes, for now. I'll follow up on what you told me, but understand this. If anything doesn't pan out, I'll be back."

She grunts in response and turns her head for a split second. I glance at her phone, trying to identify the caller. The name reads *Peanut*. I turn and head for the doorway. The front door slams shut behind me.

"Hello?" I hear her say on the other side. She couldn't wait to get back on the phone with whoever Peanut is.

As I walk down the sidewalk toward my car, something feels off. I can't place it at first, but the hairs on the back of my neck rise. Despite my training, my nerves begin to hum. Then it hits me.

People.

The street is usually crowded, but now it's completely deserted—empty except for a dark-green Chevy Lumina creeping down the road.

My hand moves to my weapon just as the passenger-side window rolls down. A long, black barrel extends outward. I recognize it instantly.

Bbblllaaat. Bbblllaaat.

Gunfire erupts. I sprint and dive behind a thick tree as bullets tear into the trunk. Wood chips explode around me as the rounds chew through the bark. I squeeze my eyes shut, praying the tree holds.

Bbblllaaat. Bbblllaaat.

Each impact sends vibrations through my body. I grip my Sig with both hands, but I'm pinned down with no clear shot. Sweat pours into my eyes, but I'm too terrified to wipe it away.

Then the tires screech. The gunfire stops.

I peek out just in time to see the Lumina disappear around the corner. My lungs burn as I struggle to breathe. Doors open, and residents pour out, scanning the street, checking to see if it was one of their own who got hit.

"Oh my God, Detective, are you okay?" Tierra cries when she spots me standing in her yard, gun lowered, body still trembling.

Instinctively, my eyes flick to the phone in her hand. *Did she set this up? Was Peanut in that car?* I don't know. And I don't trust myself to ask. I simply nod and keep walking. By the time I get into my car, the neighbors have already retreated inside. Their concern evaporated the moment they realized it wasn't one of them.

I start the engine, my pistol resting on my lap.

Someone doesn't want me to know the truth. But I won't stop until I do.

Chapter 11

"Ka'Darious, do you want to grab something to eat on the way there?"

He doesn't answer, just shakes his head.

Today, I'm taking him to see his father. Maybe Jessy can reach him, because I clearly can't. Even though I forbade him from wearing red in my car, he's still draped in it: a red Coogi shirt with matching shorts, red-and-white Retro 13 Jordans, and red-and-white socks.

I don't understand why he feels the need to join a gang. I make good money. Even as a single parent, my kids had everything they needed growing up.

His childhood wasn't like the boys who joined gangs because they were abandoned, starving, or trapped in poverty, the ones who had no family and saw gangs as the only way out; Ka'Darious grew up in a decent neighborhood and went to a decent school. Hell, the clothes and shoes he has on right now, I bought them. He never had to sit in the dark because the lights were cut off, and he never knew hunger because food stamps got sold for dope.

Like my mother did.

We pull up to the unit and go through the necessary searches that always feel intrusive, even though we do worse at the department. After getting cleared, we head to the front desk. I hand over the visitation slip, along with my ID. The officer takes one look at the inmate name and says, "Oh, you're here for Frazier."

The way she says it lets me know she's not too pleased about it. Then she looks at Ka'Darious. "Is this his son?" she asks, sounding confused.

"Yes, that's *his* son," I reply with more bite than intended. It seems my baby daddy is real popular with the women up here. I glance at her name tag. *Hall.*

She's brown-skinned, short, and sort of cute if you're into country bumpkins. After giving us the go-ahead, Ka'Darious and I make our way to the visitation room.

"I need some quarters so I can get Dad some snacks," he says eagerly.

I hand him the bag of quarters, and he heads straight for the vending machines.

By the time he comes back with the snacks, Jessy is being escorted in, looking fine as hell. His prison whites are tailored perfectly to his physique. His taper fade is immaculate, waves spinning. He sees me and smirks, but when his eyes land on his son, his whole face lights up.

Ka'Darious jumps up to hug him. "Boy, your ass almost as big as me," Jessy says. It's far from true, but it still makes Ka'Darious blush. *He adores his father.*

Then Jessy looks at me. "So what? I can't get a hug?"

I'm still a little salty about the female guard, but I stand up and give him one.

The moment his arms wrap around me, I melt. I want him between my thighs so bad, stroking the stress out of me until I scream his name.

"You smell good," he says as we separate. "Chanel?"

"Your favorite," I confirm.

"Hmm." He grunts as we sit back down.

I let the two of them catch up before getting into what I came to say. I don't want to shift the mood too early.

They talk about Ka'Darious's grades, his love life, and the video games he's into now. After about thirty minutes, Jessy turns to me.

"So what about you, Unique? What's been going on?"

I tell him a little about the case I'm working on, not enough to get myself in trouble, but I do tell him I believe the man in custody is innocent. I can tell he appreciates that I'm not like most of my colleagues, that I actually care about getting it right. I'm not soft on crime, but I'm not down with locking up the wrong person just to pad my stats.

He studies me. "What's really good, U? I can tell you got something on your chest, so just say it." *He knows me too well.*

I look at Ka'Darious. My first instinct is to excuse him so I can talk to Jessy alone. Instead, I decide to let him hear it. If he's man enough to join a gang, he's man enough to hear the truth. "I need to talk to you about your son."

Ka'Darious sighs and smacks his lips.

Jessy looks at him, then back at me. "What the hell is going on?" he asks.

"Well, your son has decided to join a gang."

The words hit Jessy like a slap. He looks at Ka'Darious, waiting for an explanation. Ka'Darious keeps his head down, unable to meet his father's eyes.

"What is she talking about, KD?"

When Ka'Darious stays quiet, Jessy realizes he doesn't want to speak in front of me. "U, can you give us a few? Let me see what's going on."

"Sure." I stand up and head toward the restroom. My bladder's been acting up anyway.

As I squat over the toilet seat, two women enter the bathroom.

"Girl, I need to talk Snook into sending me five hundred," one of them says. "I need my brakes fixed, and I'm a little short on rent."

"I know that's right. Girl, am I trippin', or was that Jessy's fine ass out there?" the other one asks.

"Yeah, that's him. Snook said he had a visit this weekend. That's why you couldn't come see him yourself."

"So who's that at the table with him?"

My ears perk up.

"Might be his brother or his son."

"He's a kid, so somebody had to bring him up here."

"Probably Jessy's baby mama."

"Hope so. I wanna finally see what she look like, what type of taste he got. He said she a cop or something like that."

"Well, she needs to—"

Their voices fade as they leave the restroom.

I'm pissed. Not only has he been having some woman come up here to see him, but she knows my business. I wipe up, wash my hands, and take a moment to collect myself before heading back out. The last thing I need is to cause a scene.

When I step back into the visitation area, I see Jessy talking sternly to our son. Unlike with me, Ka'Darious isn't talking back. He's listening, nodding, taking it in. Subconsciously, I scan the room for the women from the restroom. It doesn't take long to spot them. Two women sit at a nearby table, one light-skinned and one brown. Each is visiting someone, but neither can keep their eyes off our table. *I wonder which one is messing with Jessy.*

The brown-skinned one watches him especially closely. I give her a small smirk before sitting down. Jessy clearly didn't want me hearing his conversation with Ka'Darious, because the moment I sit, they stop talking.

He looks up and notices my shift in energy. "What's wrong with you?"

"Ka'Darious, can you excuse us? I need to talk to your daddy real quick."

He stands and heads toward the vending machines. Once he's out of earshot, I lean in. "Jessy, who the hell is that woman over there?"

"Over where?"

"Behind you, to the left. The brown-skinned one."

He glances back. Something subtle passes between them. He looks like he's about to lie, but then his face settles.

"She's a friend. Why?"

"A friend? Then why the hell does she know my business?"

"Your business? She doesn't know your business."

"Like hell she don't. She knows I'm in law enforcement."

"Okay, and so do hundreds of other people. That's public record, Uniquha."

I open my mouth, then close it. I don't have solid footing. I expected him to lie, but his honesty knocks the wind out of me. The truth is, I'm mad because there's another woman giving him something I won't or can't. Even if she can't touch him the way I can, it still stings, knowing he turns to someone else.

"Look, Jessy, I don't like your little side friends tossing my name or my job around. You never know what kind of shady shit people be into."

"Unique, what the hell are you talking about? You already said you don't want to do shit for a nigga."

"I never said that, Jessy. Don't put words in my mouth."

"You might not have said it, but your actions did. I've been trying to get you to really be there, and you always got an excuse."

"So my job and my freedom mean nothing to you? How the fuck am I supposed to feed your kids if I'm unemployed, or worse, sitting in jail?"

My voice shakes with anger. I'm so heated I could slap the taste out of his mouth. How dare he act like I'm not down just because I value my career, my freedom, and my ability to provide?

"You know what, Jessy? I'm sick of this shit. I know you're in here because you were defending me, but you're not about to make me feel guilty for wanting to take care of myself and my kids. How the hell am I supposed to bring them up here if I'm locked up right beside you?"

"There you go, getting all dramatic. That's your problem. You don't trust me. You think I'd put you in a position where you could lose everything. What type of nigga would I be? *That's* the problem. Not that you're scared to lose your job or your freedom, but that you don't trust me enough to know I'd never let that happen. Even though I lost my freedom behind you."

He stands, walks over to his son, and pulls him into a hug. After a few quiet, parting words, Jessy exits the visitation room.

I don't know what to think. I don't understand how he can't see things from my perspective. I catch the smug look on his little *friend's* face, but I refuse to let it get to me. Instead, I gather my son and head toward the parking lot with my head held high.

No matter how he feels, I cannot jeopardize myself just to make him feel secure. If he can't appreciate what I'm doing now, then I'll stop doing it. As Ka'Darious and I pull out of the unit, I glance in my rearview mirror, unsure when I'll ever see it again.

Halfway home, my phone rings. I check the caller ID. It's my security company.

"Hello?"

"Ms. Gordon, this is Bridgett from Mango Security Company. Is everything okay at your home? We received an alert that your alarm was triggered and failed to reset."

"I'm not home. I'm about an hour away."

"Would you like us to alert the authorities?"

"Yes. Yes, of course." My mind starts racing. The first thing I think about is Rachel's diary. Thankfully, it's in my work bag, locked in my trunk.

Maybe it's Shantel coming home and forgetting the code. I doubt it. The code is her dad's birthday.

I call Carter and fill him in. Then I look over at Ka'Darious. He's only caught bits and pieces of the conversation. "I'm taking you to your granny's house." Surprisingly, he doesn't protest.

"Okay. Whatever."

The conversation with his father must've humbled him.

Less than an hour later, we pull up to my mother's house in Lakewood. Gloria Gordon, former department store manager, grieving widow, recovering addict, and now a loving mother and grandmother. She's been clean for years now.

At first, I was skeptical. She'd tried to quit before and relapsed every time. But once she made it past a year and a half sober, I knew she had a real chance.

I pull into the driveway and notice her boyfriend, Mr. Clifton's, car parked out front. She was hesitant to introduce him at first, afraid I'd reject him out of loyalty to my dad. I reassured her that Dad would want her happy, and so do I. Mr. Clifton is a big reason she got clean and stayed that way. I can't do anything but respect that.

Ka'Darious and I climb the short set of steps. Mr. Clifton opens the door. He's short, potbellied, with a jovial smile and deep dimples.

"Hey, Unique. Ka'Darious. What brings y'all by?" he asks, stepping aside to let us in.

"Just dropping KD off," I say as we enter. The sweet aroma of pecan pie hits me immediately, making my stomach growl. "I see Momma's at it again," I say.

Mr. Clifton smiles. Once Ka'Darious settles onto the couch, I turn to leave. I'd love to stay, but I need to get back to the house and see what's going on. Just as I reach the door, I hear Ka'Darious say, "Hey, Shantel."

I freeze and turn slowly. Shantel is standing in the living room. One look at how she's dressed tells me she's been staying here. For how long, I don't know. She doesn't even look at me. She hugs her brother, then disappears into the spare room. I head straight for the kitchen.

"Momma, why didn't you tell me Shantel was here?"

My momma slips the wooden spoon into the pot and calmly says, "Because she asked me not to. Did you want me to break my granddaughter's trust?"

"But Ma, I was worried sick about her," I whine.

She sighs heavily. "I know, and I understand. But she called Ka'Darious every day."

That's why he didn't protest about coming over here. He knew his sister was safe.

I'm about to say more when my phone starts ringing. It's Carter.

"Hello?"

"I'm over at your house, and it doesn't look good. Someone ransacked it. They were clearly looking for something. There's stuff everywhere. Drawers pulled out. Mattresses flipped."

"I'm on my way," I say before hanging up.

I look at my mother and pinch the bridge of my nose. "I don't have time to deal with this right now, but you and I will finish this conversation later. Someone broke into the house, and I need Ka'Darious to stay here. At least until Monday morning."

"Child, you know my grandbabies can stay here as long as they need."

I spot a freshly baked pecan pie cooling on the counter and give her a look. She laughs. "Girl, go ahead."

I cut myself a generous slice and take it with me.

Back in the living room, Ka'Darious is too busy on his phone to say goodbye. I acknowledge Mr. Clifton instead and head out.

When I pull up to my house, I see two squad cars, Carter, and our unmarked parked along the street. One look at his face tells me it's bad. The moment I step out, he fills me in. "It looks like a hurricane hit. I don't know what they were searching for, but it had to be more than one person."

As soon as I step inside, I see he's right—couch cushions overturned, kitchen drawers dumped onto the floor. The bedroom is worse. There are clothes everywhere, and mattresses were flipped. One person couldn't have done this alone in such a short time. This was coordinated. I'm pretty sure I know what they were looking for. The only question is why. *There must be something very damaging in that diary.*

Carter finds me standing there, clutching a handful of panties. The violation settles heavily in my chest.

"Gordon, you might want to start thinking about installing cameras."

I've always been against cameras. I don't trust tech companies or the people behind the screens watching them. But standing in the wreckage of my home, imagining Ka'Darious here, alone, makes me shiver. "Maybe you're right," I admit. "I'll look into it."

He helps me pick up what he can.

After filing a quick report, I dismiss the uniforms. Once we're alone, Carter finally addresses the elephant in the room.

"You think this has something to do with the Willis case?"

"Of course. Ever since it became clear I was pursuing other suspects, strange things have been happening."

"Strange like what?"

I realize I never told him about being followed, about feeling watched, or about nearly getting killed after seeing Tierra Mason. I finally tell him everything.

Carter looks genuinely hurt. "Why didn't you tell me all this was going on? I would've never let you do this alone."

"And that's exactly why I didn't," I tell him. "First, I didn't want you catching heat from the brass for helping with an investigation that was officially closed. Second, it's already hard enough, getting people to talk to me. I grew up in the same environment as them. No offense, but bringing a blue-eyed White man would've shut those doors completely."

He's still hurt, but he's smart enough to understand my reasoning.

"Well, you need to be careful. Matter of fact, now that I know the dangers involved, there's no way I'm letting you continue this investigation on your own."

I let out a frustrated sigh. "Look, Carter. I appreciate it. I really do. But there's no way I can allow you to risk your career by getting involved. At least not out in the open. If you want to watch my six, I'll take that, but it has to be from a distance. If things go left, I don't need any heat coming down on you."

He wants to argue but wisely decides not to. He's been around me long enough to know this is nonnegotiable. Trying to change my mind would only start a fight.

Knowing he needs to get back to work, I shoo him off and spend the rest of the day putting my house back together. Once everything is in place and the clutter is gone, I pour myself a drink and draw a bath.

Lying in the tub, I reflect on how chaotic my life has become. Nothing seems to be going right. My kids. Jessy. My own supervisors. I'm mentally exhausted. Somewhere between the steam and the silence, I doze off.

My phone buzzes, startling me awake. I check the screen. *Unknown number.*

I get out of the tub, wrap myself in a robe, grab the diary, and spend the next couple of hours decoding more of Rachel's final days. Since I'm off tomorrow, I plan to use my time wisely.

Two hours in, I come across a passage that stops me cold.

Dear Diary,

Today something strange happened. Ed and I were out having lunch when we spotted a young Black male who was obviously a gang member. I know this because I've seen him around Barrett Station whenever I go see Gerald. I'm pretty sure he's one of Cam's friends and was there when I was assaulted. Imagine my surprise when Ed excused himself to go talk to him. I was terrified. I had no idea what they discussed, and when I saw Ed heading back to our table, I almost bolted out of the restaurant. But he returned calm as ever. If I didn't know any better, I would've thought he just went to the restroom.

I read the passage three times, hoping it would reveal something new.

What could Ed have going on with a Crip that would make him excuse himself in the middle of lunch with his wife?

There's only one way to find out, and that's to ask him myself. This time, I'm definitely bringing Carter.

Chapter 12

I lock up and head over to my mom's house. I know she and Mr. Clifton have church this morning, so the kids should be there alone.

With Gloria Gordon, if you're under fifteen, church is mandatory. Once you hit that age, she gives you what God gave everyone else. *Free will.*

I pull up, already dreading this visit. I still haven't spoken to Shantel since she stormed out. I don't park in the driveway, because I know I'll need a quick exit.

The weather is surprisingly warm, and the sun is out with a light breeze. Instead of knocking, I twist the knob and walk in.

Ka'Darious is stretched out on the couch, shirtless in basketball shorts, talking on his phone. He glances at me, sees it's me, and keeps talking. From the sound of it, he's on the phone with a girl.

I head to the kitchen to see if there's any pie left. When I come back into the living room, Shantel is standing by the window. She must've heard the car pull up. When she sees it's mine, her shoulders slump, and she shakes her head.

When she turns around, our eyes lock. It looks like she wants to say something, but instead, she tries to slip past me toward the room.

I block her path. "Shantel, we need to talk."

"About what?" she snaps. "You already said everything you needed to say."

"No, I didn't. Look. I apologize for how I acted and what I said, but you have to take accountability for your part. What you did was highly disrespectful to me, but more importantly, to yourself."

"You act like I was doing it in the house," she actually fixes her lips to say.

I want to slap some sense into her, but I take the more civil approach. I pinch the bridge of my nose and sigh. "Shantel, you're grown. Who you choose to sleep with is your business, but have some discretion. The last thing a mother wants to see is her baby girl with some man's penis in her mouth. Maybe one day, when you become a mother, you'll understand."

At the mention of her being a mother, she lifts her head. I can tell she's dying to tell me something. My heart begins to race. *No, no, no. Please don't let it be that,* I chant silently, watching my nineteen-year-old daughter struggle to find the words.

She closes her eyes and gathers herself. When she opens them again, her lips part, and the words tumble out. "I'm pregnant."

My heart drops straight to my stomach. My knees weaken, and I have to grab the back of the sofa to steady myself. If I don't, I know I'll fall flat on my face. "Say what? Please don't tell me that, Shantel." I shake my head, trying to make it disappear. "You were supposed to finish college."

"I don't think I'll keep it," she interrupts.

My jaw nearly hits the floor. I believe in abortion under certain circumstances, but killing a life because you were careless has never sat right with me. "Shantel, you know how I feel about—"

"Momma, no offense, but this isn't your decision to make."

My lips form a hard line as I force myself to stay quiet. "What did Mayo have to say about it?" I finally ask.

She looks away. *He doesn't know.* "Well, I don't know if it's his," she admits.

"What the hell?" I look up at the ceiling. "Lord, have mercy," I mutter under my breath. I want to lecture her about morals and principles, about protection and sticking to one man. But how can I? I take a breath. "Look, Shantel. You're right. It's your body and your decision. But regardless of who the father is, that's my grandchild. Choosing to end an innocent life would be the most selfish thing you could do." Just to drive it home, I add, "What if I had chosen to abort you or your brother because I messed up and didn't know who the father was?"

Shantel shakes her head, shame washing over her face. Tears slide down her cheeks. I pull her into a tight embrace as she breaks down.

"I'm so sorry, Momma."

"Ssshhh. It's okay, baby girl. I know. I know. You're not alone. We're all in this with you," I tell her, rubbing her back. When she finally calms down, I pull back and hold her at arm's length, looking her straight in the eyes. "No matter what happens, remember this. We are strong women. I raised you and your brother after your dad went to jail, with all that time. And we made it work, didn't we?"

She nods, understanding settling in. *She'll see this through. That's what real women do.*

When I get ready to leave, they both assume they're coming with me. I have to stop them.

"The house was broken into."

"What do you mean, broken into?" Ka'Darious asks, finally putting his phone down.

"Someone ransacked the place."

They exchange worried looks.

"What did they take?" Shantel asks.

"Nothing. Whatever they were looking for, they didn't find." Of course, I don't tell them I know exactly what the burglars were after. The less they know, the better.

I go over the itinerary for the day. First, Carter and I need to comb through Mandy's phone transcripts again and see if we can pull something new from who she was corresponding with in her final days. Then, I have to go visit Ed Willis and find out what kind of business he has with a known gang member, who also just so happens to know his wife was having an extramarital affair. Once I get myself together, I grab my things and head out the door.

When I step outside, I notice my neighbors are once again getting ready to go somewhere. Daisy's luggage is packed and stuffed into the trunk of their Benz. Art and I lock eyes for the briefest moment before my gaze shifts to her.

"Hey, girl! Y'all headed somewhere?" I ask.

"My mother's ill, so I'm heading to California for a week to help take care of her."

She's the only one going.

Art stands directly behind her. I resist the urge to look his way, even though I wonder if he's thinking the same thing I am. *We have a week.*

"Well, I'll be praying for her. Have a safe trip," I say, sliding into my car.

The entire drive to work, my thoughts drift into territory they shouldn't. I know sleeping with another woman's husband is wrong on every level, but I still find myself hoping that all the criminals I put away somehow balance out the bad.

I arrive at headquarters twenty minutes later. Carter is already in his office, deep into the transcripts. When he sees me, his eyes light up.

"Hey, G, take a look at this," he says, handing me three sheets of paper. "Tell me what you see."

At first, nothing jumps out. Then I realize I'm forcing it. I relax and let the words flow instead of hunting them. That's when it hits me. I look up at Carter, who gives me a knowing smile.

I rush back to my office and grab my half of the transcripts. The same patterns show up again, but this time, I catch something new: a reference to a book. The caller wanted Mandy to read a book called *The Majestic Ringer* and "do what the main character does."

I snatch the pages and hurry back to Carter. We both feel it immediately, that moment when you know you've stumbled onto something important. I download the book to my phone and skim through it as fast as I can.

In the story, the main character meets her secret lover at a snow cone shop down the street from her house. There's only one snow cone shop on this side of town, and it's within a thirty-mile radius of the apartments where Mandy lived. Once we pinpoint the location, Carter and I practically trip over each other, trying to get out of the building and into the car.

Jack Frost Snow Palace sits on a lot off Normandy. As soon as we pull up, I understand why the suspect chose this spot. The small Mom-and-Pop shop has absolutely no surveillance. It's a little more than a hut with picnic tables and benches outside. Being that it's winter, the shop is closed.

I smack the dashboard in frustration, then something clicks. "Drive to the nearest business," I tell Carter.

He does, and we end up across the street at a music performance shop that sells subwoofers, radios, and car accessories.

Carter looks at me, slightly confused. Even with their cameras, it's almost impossible to see the snow cone stand from that angle. Still, he trusts my instincts. We park, get out, and head inside.

The shop isn't crowded, but business is steady. Behind the counter stands a skinny, twenty-something Black kid with a mini fro, acne across his face, and braces on his teeth. His name tag reads *Kenny.*

"Welcome to Sound Empire," he says. "How can I help you today?"

"How are you doing, Kenny? I'm Detective Gordon, and this is Detective Carter. We need to ask you a few questions about an incident that occurred almost a month ago."

Kenny immediately looks nervous. He's probably worried about a weed stash in his car or something just as minor. "Uh, sure. What's it about?"

"How long have you been working for Sound Empire?" Carter asks.

"Since I was sixteen. I'm twenty now, so four years," Kenny says proudly.

"Do you remember seeing this girl anywhere around the store, or maybe across the street?" I pull out a photo of Mandy and hold it up. It's a Hail Mary, but sometimes, that's exactly what gets the job done.

Kenny studies the picture for a second. "Yeah, I've seen her, but it wasn't in here."

Carter and I both straighten up.

Kenny pulls out his phone and scrolls through his gallery. "A couple weeks ago, I helped this dude install his system, some high-performance twelves with a 3400-watt amp. After we finished, I told him I wanted to make a video for my Gram."

He finds what he's looking for, presses play, and turns the phone toward us.

What we see makes my stomach drop.

In the background of the video, Mandy is sitting on one of the benches across the street, waiting. A car pulls up. She spots it immediately, jumps up with excitement, and walks over. The driver steps out, hugs her, and she climbs into the passenger seat.

A wave of sickness floods me. *This nasty motherfucker.*

"Something didn't feel right about him," I say as we rush back to the precinct.

Carter is already on the phone, trying to secure a search warrant for the suspect's home, when my phone vibrates in my pocket. At the same time, the radio crackles. I grab the CB.

"Gordon here."

"We have a possible one eight seven at 300 Uvalde," the dispatcher says.

A chill runs through me. That's where Steven lives.

I confirm that we're en route, then glance at my phone. It's Shantel. She's called three times in less than a minute.

Something is wrong.

I call her back, and she answers immediately.

"Hello? Hello? Momma, where are you?" she rushes out.

"Slow down, Shantel. What's wrong?"

"I don't know. I was on the phone with KD when I heard gunshots. Then the call dropped. He hasn't answered since."

My heart skips, and my head starts to spin. I whisper a prayer under my breath. *Lord, please protect my son.*

"Was he with Steven?" I ask, already knowing the answer.

"I think so. That's who came to pick him up from Granny's after school."

"Okay. I'm about to swing by there and check on him. I'm sure he's fine, so don't stress yourself," I say, even though I don't fully believe it. "I'll call you as soon as I talk to him."

I hang up before my voice can break. Carter doesn't try to console me. He knows better. In this line of work, words don't mean a damn thing, especially when it's one of your own.

We reach The Oaks in record time. Multiple plainclothes officers are already on scene. Dozens of people line the sidewalks, watching. As soon as we step out, a first responder approaches, a plainclothes detective named Alfred.

"We've got a gunshot victim. Fatal. Dead on arrival. Multiple gunshot wounds. Early assessment says the headshot was likely the kill shot."

As he speaks, my chest tightens. My lungs feel like they're collapsing while my heart pounds too hard for my body to keep up. "Where?" I manage to croak.

Carter and I follow him toward the scene. Yellow tape is already up, securing the area. At first, all I see is a body soaked in blood, dressed head to toe in red. A matching bandanna lies sprawled on the concrete beside him. My knees go weak as my worst fear threatens to come true.

As I get closer, I recognize the tattoo on the victim's forearm. God forgive me, but sudden relief overtakes me. I almost let out a giddy laugh when I realize the victim is not my son. But it easily could have been, because the young Black male lying out on the concrete is none other than his best friend, Steven.

Frantically, I look around for my baby boy. "Alfred?"

The pudgy, brown-skinned officer turns his head.

"Was there anyone else on the scene?" I ask, my voice shaking.

"Yes. I was just about to tell you. Apparently, his friend was with him, but he's refusing to talk."

"Where is he?" My knees weaken with relief.

Alfred points between two squad cars. There sits my son, perched on the curb with his head hanging low. I can only imagine what he's feeling right now.

Steven had become like a brother to him, the older brother he never had but always wanted. Timidly, I walk over. "Ka'Darious?"

He lifts his head. Bloodshot eyes stare up at me, full of anguish. "I'm so sorry, baby. I know y'all were really close. No one should ever have to watch their friend get murdered."

His face tightens, and his lips press together as he struggles to hold back tears. My baby boy is trying to cope the way he thinks a man should. I need him to know strong men cry too. I squat beside him, pull him into me, and let him break down on my shoulder. "It's okay, Son. Let it out.

Cry for your friend. Let it all out," I whisper as his sobs soak through my jacket.

Minutes later, he finally pulls himself together and steps away from me. *Now comes the hard part.*

"Son, I know this is hard, but the only way we can put whoever did this behind bars is if you help us. We need you to tell us exactly—"

"I'm not doing no snitching, Momma." His words hit me like a slap. I've never taught Ka'Darious that giving information to the police is wrong. That 'no snitching' mentality didn't come from me.

"So, you're willing to let whoever did this walk free? Someone who killed the person you looked up to like a brother?" I hate using interrogation tactics on my own child, but I don't see another way.

Something shifts in his eyes. A hard resolve settles over him.

"They won't get away with it," he says quietly, then stands and walks off.

"Ka'Darious. Ka'Darious!" I call after him, but he's already gone, disappearing around the corner.

I want to chase him, but my duty is here. He needs time to grieve. He isn't thinking clearly yet.

I return to the scene where Carter is documenting evidence. I look at Steven again. Just above his right eye is a gaping hole, crushed inward from a high-powered round. *He was just in my living room a few days ago.*

Now he's lying in the middle of the street, dead before he was even old enough to drink. The sad part is, we'll be lucky if anyone cooperates. It's like people want this senseless violence to keep going.

Once the medical examiner removes the body and everything is bagged and tagged, Carter and I head back to the precinct. I've seen dozens of homicides in my career, but this one hit differently. Outside of my father, I've never had personal ties to a victim. This boy had been in my home. He was my son's friend.

Back at the station, we sign in the evidence. While waiting for the warrant, Carter and I go back over everything related to the Amanda case. The more I analyze it, the clearer things become.

An hour later, the search warrant finally comes through.

We head straight to Mr. Thomas's house.

As soon as we pull up, I spot the same dark-green Toyota Camry from the surveillance video sitting in the driveway. A tow truck is already en route to seize the vehicle. We're hoping to find DNA that will irrefutably tie him to Mandy's murder.

Knock, knock, knock.

Seconds later, Vince answers the door, wearing plaid shorts and a worn Metallica T-shirt. The moment he sees us, his eyes go dull. *He knows we've discovered what he's done.*

"Wh-what's this about, officers?"

I don't respond. Instead, I present the warrant and step inside, forcing entry. "Bag up the computer, the phone, and any other electronic devices he can communicate on. Also collect linens, clothing, and anything DNA can be located on."

The plainclothes officers and forensic techs immediately get to work.

Vince Thomas stares blankly at the warrant as if it's written in a foreign language. I turn back to him. "Mr. Thomas, we need to ask you a few questions. At this time, you are not under arrest. But you can help yourself by being truthful. You don't have to speak to us, but if the evidence comes back the way I believe it will, nothing you say later will save you."

He looks around his small home as his belongings are bagged, tagged, and boxed up. "Okay," he mutters.

I glance at Carter, and he nods.

Outside, the tow truck lifts the Camry onto the flatbed. We place Vince in the back of the sedan and head to the precinct.

During the drive, I fight the urge to unload every question in my head. This man is a special kind of sick, the kind I take real satisfaction in removing from the streets. If I were honest with myself, I'd admit I want to pull over and put a bullet in his head.

At headquarters, Carter places him in an interrogation room. I grab still shots from the video Kenny emailed me and head inside.

Vincent Thomas sits hunched over the table. His right leg bounces uncontrollably. I spread the photos across the table. "I need you to explain why a student is getting into your car on a weekend. The same weekend she just happens to go missing."

He glances at the pictures and grimaces. He knows he's done. There's no reasonable explanation, but I want to see if he's foolish enough to try.

For half a minute, silence hangs heavily in the room. Finally, he exhales. "She was my friend," he says.

"A friend? What kind of friend?" I keep my tone even. You don't rush a confession. You guide it. Guilt does the rest.

"I started tutoring her in English, then…" He trails off and looks at me, searching for sympathy.

I swallow my disgust. "Then what?"

"It became something more. Look, Detective. I cared about her. I really did. I know it was wrong, but it wasn't my intention. It just happened, and before I knew it, we went too far."

"Is that why you killed her? Because things went too far, and you didn't want anyone finding out?"

Vincent shakes his head and opens his mouth to speak when the interrogation room door swings open.

"Vincent, don't say another word."

A skinny White man with brown hair and a hooked nose enters, dressed in Armani and carrying a Louis Vuitton briefcase.

"Daniel, what are you doing here?" Vincent asks, surprised.

The lawyer sets his briefcase down. "Your neighbor, Phil, saw you get arrest—"

"Detained," I cut in.

He shoots me a look of pure contempt before turning back to Vincent. "Phil called your mother, and she called me." Then he looks at me again. "This interview is over. Unless you have grounds to arrest him, my client and I are leaving."

"Well, technically, he just admitted to having sexual relations with an underage female who was also his student," I reply calmly. "That alone carries up to twenty years and mandatory lifetime registration. Teaching is the least of his worries."

Technically, I'm bluffing. Even though he alluded to having sex with Mandy, he never actually said the words. I don't want to overplay my hand, so I make it seem like I'm cutting him a break.

"Even though I could hit you with charges based on that alone, I won't," I tell him. "Make no mistake, if any incriminating DNA evidence comes back, we're coming for you, Vincent."

That part isn't a bluff.

I step aside and watch Vince and his lawyer get up and walk out. Seconds after they leave, Carter enters.

"That bastard killed her to keep a scandal from coming out," he says. "He practically admitted it. If his mouthpiece hadn't walked in, we would've had an ironclad confession."

He isn't wrong. Even though we missed the layup, we still have a solid mid-range shot. I'm pretty confident something will come back from the DNA analysis.

So, Mandy was Vincent's secret lover.

Something clicks. I rush back to my office and dig through the Willis file. An idea starts forming, but first, I call Carter and tell him we need to pay Ed a visit. He's ready without hesitation. Fifteen minutes later, we're out the door.

As we turn onto Ed Willis's street, a dark-blue luxury sedan pulls off ahead of us. Two Black males sit in the front seat. The heavy tint makes it hard to see their faces, but I know the streets well enough to tell they aren't suburban types. I feel their cold stares as they pass and turn the corner.

We pull up to Ed's house just as he's stepping outside, locking the door behind him. He's dressed in a yellow parka, boots, and a bucket hat. It's obvious he's heading out to fish. He notices our unmarked car and pauses.

"How you doing, Ed?" Carter greets him as we step out.

Ed glares at me, clearly irritated that I'm still working his wife's case. *Get in line.*

"How are you, Detective?" he asks. "As you can see, I'm heading out, fishing."

"This won't take long," Carter replies. "We just wanted to touch base on something we recently learned about your wife's murder."

Ed finally looks directly at me. "Is this both of you, or just you, Detective Gordon?"

Before I can answer, Carter steps in. "It's both of us, Ed. We understand you want closure. As a decorated former officer, I'd hope you can respect our pursuit of justice. We want to make sure we put the right man away."

Ed snorts. I can't help but wonder how many innocent people he locked up just to say he closed a case.

After a moment, he nods. "Alright. Come in. I can spare ten or twenty minutes."

We follow him inside. The first thing I notice is what's missing. Every photo of Rachel has been taken down. *Just like at Tierra and Gerald's house.*

"So, what's this about?" he asks, settling into his recliner.

"We recently learned that during a lunch you and your wife had, a couple of gang members showed up," I say. "Gang members that you excused yourself to speak with."

Shock flashes across his face. He wasn't expecting that.

"We believe those same gang members, or someone connected to them, may be responsible for your wife's murder."

I leave out the part about Rachel's affair with a man tied to the same gang.

Ed squints at us. "Who told you that?"

"We came across evidence that led us there," I reply smoothly. "We followed up and verified its authenticity." A bold lie, but a necessary one. "We just need you to tell us who those gang members were and what kind of business you had with them that day."

Ed looks at us, exasperated. "This is ridiculous. My wife gets murdered, and you're asking me about a couple of good-for-nothing gang bangers who interrupted our lunch months ago? Well, if you must know, they were there for Rachel."

Now it's me who can't hide my surprise.

"Look, detectives. I don't want what I'm about to tell you ending up in the press. Rachel had a pill problem. Those guys were her pushers. She ran up a pretty high tab. When she found out she was pregnant, she stopped using, but she also cut back on her hours at work. Those dudes figured out where we were having lunch and crashed it, so to speak. Before they caused a scene, I pulled them to the side and paid them off."

I study Ed closely as he recounts his version of events. He doesn't show any signs of dishonesty or deception. Then again, he's a seasoned former officer and would know exactly what to look for. "Would it be too much to ask if you remembered their descriptions?" I ask.

"I'm not even sure I could pick them out in a lineup. It was a very brief encounter. The bill was eight hundred. I paid them an even thousand to settle it and never deal with her again. As soon as they left the restaurant, I forgot all about it."

Frustration starts to settle in. Once again, someone is contradicting how Rachel described events. *Was she mentally ill?* A person would have to be to write lies in a diary meant only for themselves. It feels like I'm going in circles. Every time I take a step forward, something knocks me back.

Ed's phone vibrates. He lifts a finger, signaling he needs to take the call. "Yeah, I'm just about to walk out the door," he says as he stands and heads toward the front.

Carter and I take the hint, stand, and meet him at the doorway. He shakes Carter's hand first, then lowers the phone and says, "Alright, Detectives. Sorry I couldn't be more help." Then he shakes my hand. His grip is surprisingly strong—too strong, like he's trying to make a point. I don't let it rattle me. I smile and return the gesture.

As Carter and I get back into the car, a sense of unease settles over me. I don't know what else to do. Time is slipping away, and I'm no closer to finding the killer.

"How's Ka'Darious holding up?" Carter asks, pulling me from my thoughts.

"Honestly, I don't know. I've been calling him, but it's straight to voicemail. Maybe when I get home tonight, I can talk to him face-to-face."

"I know that's tough. Being fifteen and watching your best friend get murdered in front of you…" Carter says quietly.

My father's murder flashes through my mind. Even though I didn't see it happen, it still shaped my entire life. "Yeah, it is," I reply. "I just hope he helps us put the ones responsible away instead of trying to handle it himself."

"Right," Carter agrees.

We pull up to the precinct just as the sun begins to set. I'm about to get out when Carter stops me. "Unique, go ahead and head home so you can check on your son. I'll hold things down here."

I want to protest out of duty, but my first responsibility is my family. "You sure?"

"Of course." The way he says it tells me he wishes he had done the same more often.

"I appreciate that," I say as I step out and head to the trunk. Since the break-in, I don't let the diary out of my sight.

A sharp cold cuts through me as a strong gust of wind smacks my face. *I'll be glad when winter's over.*

I unlock my car door and slide inside. Immediately, I know something's wrong. It's subtle, but someone has been in my vehicle. A familiar fragrance lingers, teasing my senses, but I can't place it.

Someone I've been in contact with recently was here.

My anger begins to bubble. The level of disrespect is insurmountable. I grab my pistol from the holster, set it on my lap, crank the engine, and head out.

On the way home, a sudden thought hits me. Instead of continuing to my house, I make a detour toward Cam's apartment. The last time I was over there, I was abducted and almost killed. *I won't make the same mistake twice.*

As I turn into the complex, dozens of bodies are loitering around: drug addicts, dealers, and even kids playing tackle football in the grassy areas. I park in front of the building across from Cam's, positioning myself where I have a clear view of his front door. I'm not exactly sure what I'm looking for, but my intuition tells me to be patient. *It will come.*

I keep a watchful eye on anyone walking near my car. I don't have to wait long before Cam's door swings open. He steps out dressed in royal blue from head to toe. The brim of his Kansas City Royals hat is pulled low over his eyes. His neck and wrist sparkle with jewelry. *He must be heading out tonight.*

I watch as he gets into his candy-blue Cadillac SRX on twenty-four-inch rims and pulls out of the parking lot.

Seconds later, he exits the complex. I follow at a safe distance. As we turn onto Mesa Drive, I check the time. *8:32 p.m.* I decide right then that I'll spend the entire night tailing him if I have to.

He makes a few stops—first at a local pharmacy, then at the liquor store. After that, we take a very familiar route. I'm not surprised when we end up in front of Tierra's house. He parks, and I do the same.

I expect him to get out, but instead, Tierra comes bouncing out of the house. She's wearing a short, blue-and-white mini dress, four-inch heels, a Chanel bag, and gold-and-white Gucci frames. *I wonder how long this has been going on.*

I follow them all the way downtown to a restaurant called Entice. Once they go inside, I stay in the car and call Carter to brief him on what I've uncovered.

"Do you want me to come down there?" he asks.

"Nah, I got it. I'm not going to engage, only observe. Something's going on here, and I need to see exactly what it is and how it ties back to Rachel Willis's murder," I tell him before hanging up.

As I wait, my mind drifts to another time I was downtown, enjoying the nightlife. That night when my entire life changed. *The night Jessy came to my defense and killed the man I was having an affair with. The man that—*

I snap back to reality as the couple exits the restaurant hand-in-hand. Cam opens the passenger door for Tierra, and I catch a glimpse of her right calf. *A tattooed rose.* My mind flashes back to the first time I visited Cam's apartment. The woman lying in his bed, the one he shut the bedroom door on so I wouldn't see her face. The two of them have been sleeping together.

That's it. That's how she found out about Rachel. Rachel spent time with Gerald at Cam's apartment. Cam could've used that information to get close to Tierra. *That's cold-blooded.*

My heart starts racing. Now I have a solid motive for both of them. They killed Rachel and framed Gerald so they could be together.

I'm about to call Carter when my phone starts ringing in my hand. It's Carter.

"Hello?"

"Gordon, are you still in the field?"

"Yeah. Why? What's going on?"

"I just got a call about Vince Thomas."

"What about him?"

"They found him dead in his apartment about an hour ago."

"Say what?"

"Yeah. I'm heading over there right now."

"Okay. I'll meet you there."

"What about your surveillance?" he asks.

I tell him everything I've just uncovered.

"So, it's his own brother and the girlfriend," he says, sounding skeptical.

"It looks that way," I reply. "We'll talk when we meet."

"So much for taking it in early, huh?"

"Yeah. So much for that," I answer as I pull out of the restaurant parking lot, just seconds ahead of Cam and Tierra.

Chapter 13

We arrive at Vince Thomas's home, and there's already a significant amount of activity outside. The M.E. is there, along with the coroner. As we park and step out, an officer by the name of Maxwell greets us and gives a rundown of the scene.

"The neighbor, Ms. Kinsley, called and reported hearing a single gunshot around 7:35 p.m. The dispatcher advised her to stay put, but she decided to walk over and check on him anyway. She knocked, got no response, then went inside and found the victim unresponsive. Cause of death appears to be a single gunshot wound to the head."

I shake my head. "Did he leave a note?" Carter asks.

"In fact, he did."

Maxwell leads us inside. Vince Thomas is lying on his living room floor, a .357 revolver resting near his fingertips. Blood and fragments of bone are soaked into the piss-stained carpet. Maxwell walks over to the nightstand, retrieves the suicide note, and hands it to me.

I just want to apologize to Mandy's family. I never meant to hurt her. I truly loved her, even though I know I shouldn't have. I disgraced myself and my family. I pray and hope everyone can forgive me.

Hopefully, this will be enough closure for Mandy's family. I give forensic the go-ahead to bag and tag everything. Even though it appears to be a suicide, protocol still applies. You never know. Someone could have killed him and staged the scene.

While evidence is being collected, I take a moment to look around the small home. A framed photo sits on the entertainment center. Vince is out fishing, mid-catch, rod bent, hand tight on the reel as he pulls back with all his strength. *It's the same type of fishing pole Ed Willis owns.* I stare at the picture longer than I should.

"Gordon, we just got a call from headquarters. The lieutenant wants to see you," Carter says, snapping me out of it.

"Did he say why?"

"No, but he doesn't sound too happy."

"Figures," I mutter as we head back outside.

On the drive back to the precinct, my mind races through possibilities. I barely realize we've arrived until Carter opens his door and steps out. As soon as we enter the building and approach the sergeant's desk, I'm told my lieutenant wants to see me. Alone.

Carter gives me a look of support before heading to his office. I make my way down the hall and stop outside the lieutenant's door.

Knock, knock, knock.

"Come in."

I step inside to find Lt. Anders standing next to Lt. Mays's desk. "You wanted to see me?"

"Yes," Mays says. "What is this I'm hearing about you still working the Willis case?"

I glance at Anders, uneasy about discussing a homicide investigation in front of a narcotics lieutenant. Mays doesn't catch it. "I came across a key piece of evidence that points to another suspect," I explain.

Both of them perk up. "And who does this evidence point to?" Mays asks.

I glance at Anders again. This time, he gets the hint. "Anders, will you give us a moment?"

"Of course," he replies, though his tone says otherwise. "I'll catch up with you later."

He doesn't bother hiding his disdain as he brushes past me, close enough for me to catch the scent of his cologne.

Once the door closes, I ask, "What's his problem?"

"Who? Anders?" Mays shrugs. "He's alright. He just doesn't like that you're creating loopholes for the defendant to slip through. He wants justice for the family. Now, tell me about this alternate suspect. Do you have someone ready to bring in?"

"Well, no and yes," I answer carefully. "I have someone in mind, but I'm still putting the pieces together. I just need—"

"Listen, Gordon. Luckily, that Thomas character offed himself and left us a confession. Do you think that was fair to little Mandy's family? You didn't give her 100 percent of your focus."

"No, sir, it was not," I say, feeling sick about it.

"No, it was not," he repeats. "I'm giving you my last warning. If I hear of you working on this Willis case for one second longer, you'll be on suspension. Do we understand each other?"

"Yes, sir."

"Dismissed."

Just like that, the Willis case is closed. I leave his office, feeling like a failure. I'm almost certain Gerald Blackwell is innocent. But now, because of bureaucratic bullshit, he'll be convicted and more than likely sentenced to death. *This is not why I became a detective.*

I walk back to my office, grab my bag, and pull the diary out. Knowing this is the last night I'll have to dive into it, I spend the next couple of hours decoding her entries. One in particular gives me insight into just how stressful her last days were.

I think I might be losing my mind. Either that, or someone is following me. I've seen the same dark colored sedan waiting across the street when I leave the parking garage at my job. I know I've seen that car before, but I can't place where. It's appeared at least five or six times in the last couple of weeks. I tried to get a look inside, but the windows are too darkly tinted. Maybe my husband has someone following me. Or it could be Gerald's brother, or his ghetto ass girlfriend. I told Gerald, and he suggested I get a gun. I absolutely despise those things, so we compromised on a knife. I'm so scared something will happen to me and my baby.

My heart aches for this woman. To feel death breathing down your neck and not be able to stop it, not knowing from which direction it will come.

That's the last complete entry. I close the diary and head down to the evidence room to place it back in its assigned locker. I thought for sure Lt. Mays would confront me about lifting evidence, but surprisingly, he doesn't say a word. In fact, when I mentioned having evidence pointing to another suspect, he didn't even ask what that evidence was.

I lean back in my chair and close my eyes. My mind races. Clips from the past few weeks flash through my consciousness. Suddenly, something clicks. My eyes fly open. I jump up and rush to Carter's office to tell him what I've realized. While I'm there, my phone starts ringing. *It's Ka'Darious.*

"Hello?"

"Momma, I need to talk to you. It's important."

"Okay. Is something wrong?"

"It's about what happened to Steven."

I glance at Carter. "Alright, baby. I'm on my way home now. I'll see you in about thirty minutes."

"Okay." He hangs up.

"That was Ka'Darious," I tell Carter. "He wants to talk about what happened with Steven."

"That's good," Carter says. "That means his morals outweigh that street code they try to brainwash them with."

"I hope so. We'll follow up on the new lead first thing in the morning," I say, heading back to my office to grab my things.

After leaving the evidence room, I exit through the side door and head down the steps. The winter wind cuts straight through me, and my sports jacket is no match for the cold.

I pull it tighter around my body as I walk toward my car. When I get within a few feet, I notice it. A flat tire.

"What the fuck?" It doesn't look punctured, just completely flat. I definitely don't need this right now.

I shake my head and pull out my phone to call Carter for help. Suddenly, the wind carries a familiar scent, that same fragrance I noticed in my car before.

Realization hits me like a runaway train. *I know where I recognize it from.*

Smack.

A sharp pain explodes at the base of my skull. My body goes limp, and everything goes black.

Chapter 14

"Girl, this baby is kicking my ass," I told Sanders as we sat in her off-base apartment. I was two and a half months pregnant and already beginning to show. "It's a good thing we're about to discharge," I added.

I told my superior officers I slipped up and got pregnant while on leave. Even though pregnancy was frowned upon, my four years of service were almost up anyway.

"Speak for yourself. I gotta bring my black ass back in three weeks," she said, putting the finishing touches on her makeup. Sanders reenlisted for another two. She was getting ready for a date; I was staying in.

Like she could read my thoughts, she turned and looked at me. "What's going on with you and Brown?"

"What you mean?"

"You told me y'all stopped seeing each other, but he's always asking about you. Every time I see him."

I turned my head, dodging her judgmental stare. "Look, San. I'm not trying to deal with dude on that level. Whatever that was between us was supposed to be one night only. Now he talking about me leaving Jessy. I'm not about to do all that," I admitted.

Sergeant Brown and I had been going hard for months. When I found out I was pregnant with Jessy's baby, I didn't tell Brown. I knew he'd get weird about it. So, for the first couple of weeks, I carried on as if nothing had changed. Now that I was starting to show, I figured would be best to avoid him altogether.

"You wanna kick it here until I get back?" Sanders asked.

"Nah. I'm heading back to base. I'm going home tomorrow and need to get everything packed."

"I'm gonna miss your ass, girl. You know you my best friend," she said, pulling me into a hug.

Sanders and I grew close in basic training. It turned out, we had a lot in common. My mother was an addict, and her father was one too. Her mother died of cancer, and my father was murdered. She joined the military to escape. I joined to go back and make a difference.

I watched her finish getting dolled up before heading out to my car. As I reached for the door handle, I felt a presence behind me. My hand slipped into my purse, wrapping around my mace.

"It's just me," a familiar voice said.

I relaxed, then tensed up for a completely different reason. How did Brown know I was there? I turned around to face the man I'd been tangled up with for months. His hands were open, palms up. "Look, Unique. I don't know what I did, but I'm hurting right now. I need to see you," he said.

My heart tugged at his vulnerability. If I were being honest, I knew this man loved me. The problem was, I didn't love him. I was in love with someone else, a man I'd been with for almost six years—the father of my daughter Shantel and the baby growing inside me.

Still, avoiding Brown had only made things worse, so I decided to tell him the truth.

"Look. I'm pregnant."

His jaw dropped as his eyes drifted to my stomach. "Is it—"

***

Bump. Bump.

My head slams against metal, and I jolt awake. It's pitch black. My hands are cuffed behind my back. The air is thick and stale, and I hear tires rolling over asphalt.

I'm in the trunk of a car.

Panic crawls up my spine. My chest tightens, and my breathing becomes harder by the second. I'm terrified of confined spaces. My mind races as I try to think my way out of this. I shift, searching for anything I can use. Pain shoots down my right side, the blow to my head still screaming. I already know who did this. If I'm right, everything finally makes sense. Images of Shantel and Ka'Darious flood my mind. I *have* to make it out of this.

What feels like an hour passes before the car finally comes to a stop. My heartbeat quickens. I send up a silent prayer and brace myself. Heavy footsteps crunch against the gravel as someone gets out and walks toward the rear of the car.

Pop.

The trunk opens, and staring down at me with a scowl is none other than Ed Willis.

"Please. You don't have to do this," I start, but Ed isn't trying to hear it.

"Save your breath. You should've kept your head down and your nose out of it."

He grabs me by the scruff of my neck and yanks me out of the trunk. Pain shoots through my skull, courtesy of the bruise at the base of my head. I wince as my feet hit the ground. Ed grips my arms and drags me around what looks like a cabin in the middle of nowhere. His pickup truck is still loaded with fishing gear, the same fishing gear that made it click for me earlier. *Ed is ambidextrous.*

When we first interviewed him, the reels looked off, but I couldn't place why. It didn't hit me until I saw the picture of Vincent Thomas fishing with a left-handed rod. *Damn.*

I trip over a tree root and stumble forward. Ed catches me before I smash my face.

"Goddamn, Gordon. You clumsy with everything you do?"

"Come on, Ed. You don't have to do this. No one knows I'm here. Just let me go, and I swear I won't say a word to anyone."

He almost laughs. "Are you serious? That work on your perps? Of course, I can't let you go. First, you've been poking around in shit that didn't concern you. You don't think I know you figured out I'm the one who killed that filthy, slut wife of mine? Second, I just assaulted and kidnapped a detective. You know exactly what that means. No, Detective Gordon, you ain't going nowhere. There's only one way this ends, and that's with you dead and buried."

My heart twists. *Only one person knew I was onto Ed.* The thought of my partner betraying me rips through my chest.

He drags me to a clearing about fifty yards from the cabin. A metal chair sits there, along with a shovel and a hole that looks freshly dug.

My mind scrambles, searching for anything that might save me. "Ed, I don't know what you've been told, but I didn't know you killed your wife. All the evidence pointed to someone else. Even if I said you confessed, I don't have proof to back it up."

Ed shakes his head. "Doesn't matter. What's done is done. You know something? I really did love my wife. When I found out she was fucking one of the same lowlife gang members I was investigating, that hurt, but I could've gotten past it. When I found out she was pregnant with his baby, that was it." He paces as he talks. "Being a high-ranking narcotics officer, I made a lot of connections over the years. That stupid bitch never realized I had eyes on her everywhere she went. Even in the ghetto she loved so much."

That explains a lot, but I still need clarity. "So you paid to have her killed?"

He scoffs. "Hell no. Why would I give someone the chance to tell on me? I killed the conniving bitch myself. I found out she was visiting her gangbanger boyfriend and laid in wait. When she left, I followed her. Once we were alone on the highway, I shot out her back tire and pulled over to help. She saw it was me and got suspicious, wondering why I was on Highway 90 when I was supposed to be fishing. But after some bullshit talk, she bought it." His eyes darken. "When she got out the car to sit in mine while I changed her tire, I cracked her over the head with a tire iron. You know the rest, so I'll spare you the details."

He stops and looks at me. "What I can't understand is this. I handed you Blackwell on a silver platter. All the evidence pointed to him. Instead of being grateful, you kept sticking your nose where it didn't belong."

"Because I couldn't let an innocent man go to jail," I say, my voice steady despite the fear ripping through me.

Ed scoffs. "Innocent? Innocent? What does that even mean? Yeah, he didn't kill Rachel, but do you know how many other crimes he committed and got away with? How many murders he facilitated? This is penance for all the other shit we couldn't get him on." *Typical.*

Something clicks. Even though I already know the answer, I still have to ask. "So, Lt. Anders helped you cover this up?"

A small smile curls his lips. "Gordon, this is bigger than you. You should've learned by now, to be a top-tier detective, it ain't about guilty or innocent, or even right and wrong. It's about getting the job done. No matter what."

Droplets of water begin to splatter against my face. Then the clouds open up, and rain pours down hard. Ed reaches under his parka and pulls out a long-barrel, nickel-plated revolver.

My teeth start chattering. The fear of leaving my kids alone in this world closes in on me, stealing my breath. I can't stop shaking. He pulls the hammer back. I squeeze my eyes shut.

I brace myself for the fatal shot. Thunder cracks, and I flinch. The faint smell of gunpowder fills the air. I've never been shot, but this doesn't feel like it. I crack one eye open and freeze. Ed Willis is face down on the ground. The back of his head is blown open like a smashed pumpkin. *What the hell?*

My head snaps side to side, searching for whoever fired the shot. Then I see him step out of the tree line and into the clearing. My partner, Detective Carter, walks toward me with a rifle slung across his shoulder. I've never been so relieved to see another human being.

A sob of relief escapes me. Every thought of betrayal disappears. "Gordon, are you okay?"

"Yeah. I'm alright. I'm cuffed. Check him for the keys."

Carter flips Ed over, searches his pockets, and pulls out a set of handcuff keys. "How did you know I was here?" I ask as he frees me.

"When you left, you forgot your badge. I tried to catch you before you drove off. When I came outside, your car was still there, but your phone was on the ground, broken. After what you told me about Ed, I put two and two together. He said he was going fishing, so I had Wilkins in narcotics tell me where Lt. Anders' lake house was. Thank God he was dumb enough to bring you here."

The second the cuffs come off, I spring out of the chair and throw my arms around Carter. I kiss him hard, relief and adrenaline crashing through me. When I feel him tense, reality hits. I pull back fast.

"My bad, Carter. I don't know where that came from. I, … damn." The words stumble out.

"It's okay, G. I get it. You're happy to be alive. Don't worry about it," he says gently.

My heart still races as we stand in the awkward silence. *What the hell is wrong with you, Unique?*

Red and blue lights suddenly flash through the trees. I look at Carter.

"I didn't wait. I called for backup," he explains.

Within minutes, the area fills with uniforms. Lt. Anders steps into the clearing. The moment he sees Ed's body, he starts distancing himself, claiming he had no idea what Ed was doing while he was supposed to be fishing.

As he talks, a familiar scent hits my nose.

"What cologne is that?" I ask.

"Huh?"

"Your cologne. It's distinctive."

He looks at me strangely. "It's a mix. Curve and Armani Code."

"Really?" I say quietly.

He studies me for a second, then turns back to the other officers. Carter notices my expression.

"What's up, G?"

"Anders was involved," I tell him.

"What makes you say that?"

"Right before I was abducted, I smelled that same scent—his cologne. It was in my car, too, the day I noticed someone had been inside."

"Are you sure?"

"Of course, I'm sure. Think about it. This whole time I've been working the Willis case, Anders has been pushing the higher-ups to shut me down. Then he was in the office when I told Mays I had an alternate suspect. He must've assumed it was Ed and tipped him off."

Carter tugs on my sleeve, pulling me a few steps away from everyone else. "Gordon, you have to be very careful. We can't just throw accusations around, especially without proof. Did Ed say anything? Anything we can build on?"

"No," I admit. "I tried to get him to implicate Anders, but he deflected. I'm telling you, though, Carter, Anders is dirty."

"Well, until we have solid proof, you've got to keep that to yourself."

I grit my teeth, but I understand. As if he senses the conversation, Anders turns, and I swear I catch a smirk on his face. *You won't get away with this, I promise.* I send the threat silently as Carter walks me to the sedan.

As we pull off, Ka'Darious suddenly flashes across my mind: the call he made right before I was snatched. "Can I use your phone real quick?" I ask.

Carter digs in his pocket, pulls it out, and hands it to me. I dial three times and get the same result. No answer.

"Shit."

"What's wrong?"

"Ka'Darious isn't answering."

"Maybe he doesn't recognize the number."

"No. I made him and Shantel save your number for this exact reason."

"Did he say where he was?"

"The last time I spoke to him, he was at the house."

Carter doesn't say another word. He floors it, lights flashing, and we're headed toward my house at full speed.

The moment we step inside, I know Ka'Darious isn't there. The house is silent and empty. A note sits on his bed. My hands shake as I pick it up and read.

Momma,

I waited for you but you never showed. I guess that means I have to handle this on my own. You asked if I knew who killed Steven. It was some Crips. The thing is, they weren't trying to kill him. They were trying to get me. Steven pushed me out the way and saved my life. I have to do what's right. I love you. Tell Shantel I love her too.

I read it again, then crush it in my fist. The weight of failure presses down on my chest. My son is ready to throw his life away over gang nonsense. What does that say about how I raised him?

I grab the house phone and call his cell again and again. The first few times, it rings through, then it goes straight to voicemail.

Carter rushes in. "We've got a one eight seven on Highway 90. Three miles from Barrett Station."

My heart sinks. *No. No. No.* The entire drive, my nerves are shot. My hands tremble. My chest feels tight. The address they give us is the same motel Carter and I visited early in the Willis investigation.

When we pull in, there's only one uniform on scene. The door to room 357 is wide open. I don't stop to speak. I run inside.

The second I cross the threshold, my steps slow. Shock slams into me. Lying naked on the bed, riddled with gunshot wounds to the chest and head, are Cam and Tierra.

By the look of it, they were caught in the middle of something intense. Whoever did this knew exactly where they were and took them completely by surprise.

"Damn," Carter mutters, stepping in behind me. "Who would want them dead?"

I can think of only one person, but he's locked up and sitting in county. I keep that to myself.

"I'll go see Gerald tomorrow," I say quietly. "Tell him he's officially off the hook for Rachel's murder. When I tell him about Tierra and his brother, I'll watch his reaction."

"You want me to come with you?" Carter asks.

"No," I reply. "I got it."

"Okay. Well, let's wrap things up here so we can figure out what's going on with Ka'Darious."

As we finish up, one thought keeps looping through my mind. *Please don't let me arrive on a crime scene and find my son with his brains blown out—or worse, find out he's on the other side of the murder weapon.* The path he's on makes it feel like one of those outcomes is inevitable.

The second we step outside, Carter's phone starts ringing. He pulls it out, glances at the screen, then looks at me.

"Hello," Carter says.

After a brief conversation, he lowers the phone and meets my eyes.

"Who is it?" I ask, my voice thick with hope.

"It's Ka'Darious," he says quietly. "And he's in trouble."

Assisted Publishing Packages

Due to an increase in the price of services we have increased our prices. The prices below reflect the price increase as of 11/1/24.

BASIC PACKAGE **$699** Editing Cover Design Formatting	**UPGRADED PACKAGE** **$1000** Typing Editing Cover Design Formatting Upload eBooks to Amazon Upload Paperback to Amazon
ADVANCE PACKAGE **$1,400** Typing Editing (line editing/content) Cover Design Formatting Copyright Registration Proofreading Upload eBooks to Amazon Upload Paperback to Amazon	**LDP SUPREME PACKAGE** **$1,700** Typing Editing (line editing/content) Cover Design Formatting Copyright Registration Proofreading Set up Amazon Account Upload eBooks to Amazon Upload Paperback to Amazon Advertise on LDP's Amazon and Facebook Page

***

Other services available upon request.
Additional charges may apply

Lock Down Publications
P.O. Box 944
Stockbridge, GA 30281-9998
Phone: 470 303-9761
Email: lockdownpublications@gmail.com

Submission Guideline

Submit the first three chapters of your completed manuscript to ldpsubmissions@gmail.com. In the subject line add **Your Book's Title**. The manuscript must be in a Word Doc file and sent as an attachment. Document should be in Times New Roman, double spaced, and in size 12 font. Also, provide your synopsis and full contact information. If sending multiple submissions, they must each be in a separate email.

Have a story but no way to send it electronically? You can still submit to LDP/Ca$h Presents. Send in the first three chapters, written or typed, of your completed manuscript to:

LDP: Submissions Dept
P.O. Box 944
Stockbridge, GA 30281-9998

DO NOT send original manuscript. Must be a duplicate. Provide your synopsis and a cover letter containing your full contact information.

Thanks for considering LDP and Ca$h Presents.

NEW RELEASES

BLOODLINE OF A SAVAGE 1-3
THESE VICIOUS STREETS 1-3
RELENTLESS GOON 1-3
BY PRINCE A. TAUHID

THE BUTTERFLY MAFIA 1-3
BY FUMIYA PAYNE

A THUG'S STREET PRINCESS 1&2
BY MEESHA

CITY OF SMOKE 3
BY MOLOTTI

GET IT IN SLUGS 1 &2
BY B. STALL

STANDING ON HER BUSINESS 1&2
BY DG SANTANA

STEPPERS 1,2&3
THE REAL BADDIES OF CHI-RAQ
BY KING RIO

THE LANE 1&2
BY KEN-KEN SPENCE

THUG OF SPADES 1&2
LOVE IN THE TRENCHES 2
CORNER BOYS
BY COREY ROBINSON

TIL DEATH 3
BY ARYANNA

THE BIRTH OF A GANGSTER 4
BY DELMONT PLAYER

PRODUCT OF THE STREETS 1-3
BY DEMOND "MONEY" ANDERSON

NO TIME FOR ERROR
BY KEESE

MONEY HUNGRY DEMONS 1-2
BY TRANAY ADAMS

HUB CITY MENACE 1-3
BY J. WHITE

A THUGGISH PASSION 1&2
LAND OF DA HOOLIGANZ 1-4
KILLAZ ON STANDBY 1&2
BY IRA B.

FO'EVA ROLLIN 1&2
BY ASSA RAYMOND BAKER

THE LEVEL UP 1&3
BY LUXURY KING

Coming Soon from Lock Down Publications/Ca$h Presents

IF YOU CROSS ME ONCE 6
ANGEL V
By Anthony Fields

A THUGS STREET PRINCESS 3
By Meesha

CORNER BOYS 2
By Corey Robinson

THA TAKEOVER
By Keith Chandler

BETRAYAL OF A G 2
By Ray Vinci

SAVAGE FAMILY EMPIRE 1&2
SOULLESS GOON 1,2&3
THE DIRTY SIDE OF MONEY 1,2&3
By Prince

FOR MY ENEMY'S SAKE
AMBITIONS OF A SLIDER
FRESH OFF DA PORCH
By IRA B.

BY THE TRUCKLOAD 1-4
TIPPIN' THE SCALES 1-3
BAD BITCHES WIT GUNZ 3
PROBLEM SOLVED 2
By Christopher "Diesel" Hornezes

Available Now

RESTRAINING ORDER 1 & 2
By **CA$H & Coffee**

LOVE KNOWS NO BOUNDARIES 1-3
By **Coffee**

RAISED AS A GOON I, II, III & IV
BRED BY THE SLUMS I, II, III
BLAST FOR ME I & II
ROTTEN TO THE CORE I II III
A BRONX TALE I, II, III
DUFFLE BAG CARTEL I II III IV V VI
HEARTLESS GOON I II III IV V
A SAVAGE DOPEBOY I II
DRUG LORDS I II III
CUTTHROAT MAFIA I II
KING OF THE TRENCHES
By **Ghost**

LAY IT DOWN I & II
LAST OF A DYING BREED I II
BLOOD STAINS OF A SHOTTA I & II III
By **Jamaica**

LOYAL TO THE GAME I II III
LIFE OF SIN I, II III
By **TJ & Jelissa**

IF LOVING HIM IS WRONG…I & II
LOVE ME EVEN WHEN IT HURTS I II III
By **Jelissa**

PUSH IT TO THE LIMIT
By **Bre' Hayes**

BLOODY COMMAS I & II
SKI MASK CARTEL I, II & III

DEATH OF A SIDE CHICK | LO-LIFE

KING OF NEW YORK I II, III IV V
RISE TO POWER I II III
COKE KINGS I II III IV V
BORN HEARTLESS I II III IV
KING OF THE TRAP I II
By **T.J. Edwards**

WHEN THE STREETS CLAP BACK I & II III
THE HEART OF A SAVAGE I II III IV
MONEY MAFIA I II
LOYAL TO THE SOIL I II III
By **Jibril Williams**

A DISTINGUISHED THUG STOLE MY HEART I II & III
LOVE SHOULDN'T HURT I II III IV
RENEGADE BOYS 1-4
PAID IN KARMA 1-3
SAVAGE STORMS 1-3
AN UNFORESEEN LOVE 1-3
BABY, I'M WINTERTIME COLD 1-3
A THUG'S STREET PRINCESS 1&2
By **Meesha**

A GANGSTER'S CODE 1-3
A GANGSTER'S SYN 1-3
THE SAVAGE LIFE 1-3
CHAINED TO THE STREETS 1-3
BLOOD ON THE MONEY 1-3
A GANGSTA'S PAIN 1-3
BEAUTIFUL LIES AND UGLY TRUTHS
CHURCH IN THESE STREETS
By **J-Blunt**

CUM FOR ME 1-8
An LDP Erotica Collaboration

BLOOD OF A BOSS 1-5
SHADOWS OF THE GAME

TRAP BASTARD
By **Askari**

THE STREETS BLEED MURDER 1-3
THE HEART OF A GANGSTA 1-3
By **Jerry Jackson**

WHEN A GOOD GIRL GOES BAD
By **Adrienne**

THE COST OF LOYALTY 1-3
By **Kweli**

BRIDE OF A HUSTLA 1-3
THE FETTI GIRLS 1-3
CORRUPTED BY A GANGSTA 1-4
BLINDED BY HIS LOVE
THE PRICE YOU PAY FOR LOVE 1-3
DOPE GIRL MAGIC 1-3
By **Destiny Skai**

A KINGPIN'S AMBITION
A KINGPIN'S AMBITION II
I MURDER FOR THE DOUGH
By **Ambitious**

TRUE SAVAGE 1-7
DOPE BOY MAGIC 1-3
MIDNIGHT CARTEL 1-3
CITY OF KINGZ 1&2
NIGHTMARE ON SILENT AVE
THE PLUG OF LIL MEXICO 1&2
CLASSIC CITY
By **Chris Green**

A GANGSTER'S REVENGE 1-4
THE BOSS MAN'S DAUGHTERS 1-5

A SAVAGE LOVE 1&2
BAE BELONGS TO ME 1&2
A HUSTLER'S DECEIT 1-3
WHAT BAD BITCHES DO 1-3
SOUL OF A MONSTER 1-3
KILL ZONE
A DOPE BOY'S QUEEN 1-3
TIL DEATH 1-3
IMMA DIE BOUT MINE 1-6
DYING FOR LIKES
By **Aryanna**

A DOPEBOY'S PRAYER
By **Eddie "Wolf" Lee**

THE KING CARTEL 1-3
By **Frank Gresham**

THESE NIGGAS AIN'T LOYAL 1-3
By **Nikki Tee**

GANGSTA SHYT 1-3
By **CATO**

THE ULTIMATE BETRAYAL
By **Phoenix**

BOSS'N UP 1-3
By **Royal Nicole**

I LOVE YOU TO DEATH
By **Destiny J**

I RIDE FOR MY HITTA
I STILL RIDE FOR MY HITTA
By **Misty Holt**

LOVE & CHASIN' PAPER
By **Qay Crockett**

TO DIE IN VAIN
SINS OF A HUSTLA
By **ASAD**

BROOKLYN HUSTLAZ
By **Boogsy Morina**

BROOKLYN ON LOCK 1 & 2
By **Sonovia**

GANGSTA CITY
By **Teddy Duke**

A DRUG KING AND HIS DIAMOND 1-3
A DOPEMAN'S RICHES
HER MAN, MINE'S TOO 1&2
CASH MONEY HO'S
THE WIFEY I USED TO BE 1&2
PRETTY GIRLS DO NASTY THINGS
By **Nicole Goosby**

LIPSTICK KILLAH 1-3
CRIME OF PASSION 1-3
FRIEND OR FOE 1-3
By **Mimi**

TRAPHOUSE KING 1-3
KINGPIN KILLAZ 1-3
STREET KINGS 1&2
PAID IN BLOOD 1&2
CARTEL KILLAZ 1-3
DOPE GODS 1&2
By **Hood Rich**

THE STREETS ARE CALLING
By **Duquie Wilson**

STEADY MOBBN' 1-3

DEATH OF A SIDE CHICK | LO-LIFE

THE STREETS STAINED MY SOUL 1-3
By **Marcellus Allen**

WHO SHOT YA 1-3
SON OF A DOPE FIEND 1-4
HEAVEN GOT A GHETTO 1&2
SKI MASK MONEY 1&2
By **Renta**

GORILLAZ IN THE BAY 1-4
TEARS OF A GANGSTA 1/&2
3X KRAZY 1&2
STRAIGHT BEAST MODE 1&2
By **DE'KARI**

TRIGGADALE 1-3
MURDA WAS THE CASE 1-3
By **Elijah R. Freeman**

SLAUGHTER GANG 1-3
RUTHLESS HEART 1-3
By **Willie Slaughter**

GOD BLESS THE TRAPPERS 1-3
THESE SCANDALOUS STREETS 1-3
FEAR MY GANGSTA 1-5
THESE STREETS DON'T LOVE NOBODY 1-2
BURY ME A G 1-5
A GANGSTA'S EMPIRE 1-4
THE DOPEMAN'S BODYGAURD 1&2
THE REALEST KILLAZ 1-3
THE LAST OF THE OGS 1-3
By **Tranay Adams**

MARRIED TO A BOSS 1-3
By **Destiny Skai & Chris Green**

KINGZ OF THE GAME 1-7

CRIME BOSS 1-4
By **Playa Ray**

FUK SHYT
By **Blakk Diamond**

DON'T F#CK WITH MY HEART 1&2
By **Linnea**

ADDICTED TO THE DRAMA 1-3
IN THE ARM OF HIS BOSS
By **Jamila**

LOYALTY AIN'T PROMISED 1&2
By **Keith Williams**

YAYO 1-4
A SHOOTER'S AMBITION 1&2
BRED IN THE GAME
By **S. Allen**

TRAP GOD 1-3
RICH $AVAGE 1-3
MONEY IN THE GRAVE 1-3
CARTEL MONEY 1&2
By **Martell Troublesome Bolden**

FOREVER GANGSTA 1&2
GLOCKS ON SATIN SHEETS 1&2
By **Adrian Dulan**

TOE TAGZ 1-4
LEVELS TO THIS SHYT 1&2
IT'S JUST ME AND YOU
By **Ah'Million**

KINGPIN DREAMS 1-3
RAN OFF ON DA PLUG

DEATH OF A SIDE CHICK | LO-LIFE

By **Paper Boi Rari**

THE STREETS MADE ME 1-3
By **Larry D. Wright**

CONFESSIONS OF A GANGSTA 1-4
CONFESSIONS OF A JACKBOY 1-3
CONFESSIONS OF A HITMAN
CONFESSIONS OF A DOPE BOY
By **Nicholas Lock**

I'M NOTHING WITHOUT HIS LOVE
SINS OF A THUG
TO THE THUG I LOVED BEFORE
A GANGSTA SAVED XMAS
IN A HUSTLER I TRUST
By **Monet Dragun**

QUIET MONEY 1-3
THUG LIFE 1-3
EXTENDED CLIP 1&2
A GANGSTA'S PARADISE
By **Trai'Quan**

CAUGHT UP IN THE LIFE 1-3
THE STREETS NEVER LET GO 1-3
By **Robert Baptiste**

NEW TO THE GAME 1-3
MONEY, MURDER & MEMORIES 1-3
By **Malik D. Rice**

CREAM 2-3
THE STREETS WILL TALK
By **Yolanda Moore**

THE STREETS WILL NEVER CLOSE 1-3
By **K'ajji**

LIFE OF A SAVAGE 1-4
A GANGSTA'S QUR'AN 1-4
MURDA SEASON 1-3
GANGLAND CARTEL 1-3
CHI'RAQ GANGSTAS 1-4
KILLERS ON ELM STREET 1-3
JACK BOYZ N DA BRONX 1-3
A DOPEBOY'S DREAM 1-3
JACK BOYS VS DOPE BOYS 1-3
COKE GIRLZ
COKE BOYS
SOSA GANG 1&2
BRONX SAVAGES
BODYMORE KINGPINS
BLOOD OF A GOON
By **Romell Tukes**

CONCRETE KILLA 1-3
VICIOUS LOYALTY 1-3
BLOODY MONEY BAGS
By **Kingpen**

THE ULTIMATE SACRIFICE 1-6
KHADIFI
IF YOU CROSS ME ONCE 1-3
ANGEL 1-4
IN THE BLINK OF AN EYE
By **Anthony Fields**

THE LIFE OF A HOOD STAR
By **Ca$h & Rashia Wilson**

NIGHTMARES OF A HUSTLA 1-3
BLOOD AND GAMES 1&2
By **King Dream**

GHOST MOB
By **Stilloan Robinson**

HARD AND RUTHLESS 1&2
MOB TOWN 251
THE BILLIONAIRE BENTLEYS 1-3
REAL G'S MOVE IN SILENCE
By **Von Diesel**

MOB TIES 1-7
SOUL OF A HUSTLER, HEART OF A KILLER 1-3
GORILLAZ IN THE TRENCHES
OOPS CRY TOO 1&2
THE DAUGHTER OF A CARTEL BOSS
By **SayNoMore**

BODYMORE MURDERLAND 1-3
THE BIRTH OF A GANGSTER 1-4
By **Delmont Player**

FOR THE LOVE OF A BOSS 1&2
By **C. D. Blue**

KILLA KOUNTY 1-5
TENDER
By **Khufu**

MOBBED UP 1-4
THE BRICK MAN 1-5
THE COCAINE PRINCESS 1-10
STEPPERS 1-3
SUPER GREMLIN 1-4
A GANGSTA'S SON
By **King Rio**

MONEY GAME 1&2
By **Smoove Dolla**

A GANGSTA'S KARMA 1-5
By **FLAME**

KING OF THE TRENCHES 1-3
By **GHOST & TRANAY ADAMS**

BAD BITCHES WIT GUNZ 1&2
PROBLEM SOLVED
By "Christopher Diesel" Hornezes

QUEEN OF THE ZOO 1&2
By **Black Migo**

GRIMEY WAYS 1-3
BETRAYAL OF A G
By **Ray Vinci**

XMAS WITH AN ATL SHOOTER
By **Ca$h & Destiny Skai**

KING KILLA 1&2
By **Vincent "Vitto" Holloway**

BETRAYAL OF A THUG 1&2
By **Fre$h**

COUNTDOWN OF A KILLA 1&2
SEX, MURDER AND GOD 1&2
GUNS DOWN, BOTTOMS UP 1&2
By Lo-Life

THE MURDER QUEENS 1-7
By **Michael Gallon**

FOR THE LOVE OF BLOOD 1-4
By **Jamel Mitchell**

HOOD CONSIGLIERE 1&2
NO TIME FOR ERROR

DEATH OF A SIDE CHICK | LO-LIFE

By **Keese**

PROTÉGÉ OF A LEGEND 1,2&3
LOVE IN THE TRENCHES 1&2
By **Corey Robinson**

THE PLUG'S RUTHLESS DAUGHTER 1&2
By **Tony Daniels**

BORN IN THE GRAVE 1-3
CRIME PAYS
By **Self Made Tay**

MOAN IN MY MOUTH
By **XTASY**

TORN BETWEEN A GANGSTER AND A GENTLEMAN
By **J-BLUNT & Miss Kim**

LOYALTY IS EVERYTHING 1-3
CITY OF SMOKE 1-3
By **Molotti**

HERE TODAY GONE TOMORROW 1&2
By **Fly Rock**

WOMEN LIE MEN LIE 1-4
FIFTY SHADES OF SNOW 1-3
STACK BEFORE YOU SPLURGE
GIRLS FALL LIKE DOMINOES
NAÏVE TO THE STREETS
By **ROY MILLIGAN**

PILLOW PRINCESS
By **S. Hawkins**

THE BUTTERFLY MAFIA 1-3
SALUTE MY SAVAGERY 1&2

DEATH OF A SIDE CHICK | LO-LIFE

By **Fumiya Payne**

THE LANE 1&2
By Ken-Ken Spence

THE PUSSY TRAP 1-5
By **Nene Capri**

DIRTY DNA
By **Blaque**

SANCTIFIED AND HORNY
by **XTASY**

BOOKS BY LDP'S CEO, CA$H

TRUST IN NO MAN
TRUST IN NO MAN 2
TRUST IN NO MAN 3
BONDED BY BLOOD
SHORTY GOT A THUG
THUGS CRY
THUGS CRY 2
THUGS CRY 3
TRUST NO BITCH
TRUST NO BITCH 2
TRUST NO BITCH 3
TIL MY CASKET DROPS
RESTRAINING ORDER
RESTRAINING ORDER 2
IN LOVE WITH A CONVICT
LIFE OF A HOOD STAR
XMAS WITH AN ATL SHOOTER